PRAISE

"An invaluable tool for anyone and everyone in the entertainment industry. Paul's warmth and engaging personality shine forth through the unforgettable performances. You will gain insight and inspiration from this important work."

Yechiel Spero, *Author*

"The very embodiment of the term crooner. Knows his way round the ivories better than most, with an unbeatable repertoire of originals and classics to keep you entertained."

Alex Clare, *Island Records artist*

"He speaks in a distinctive Scottish accent. With a friendly, bubbly personality that lights up the room and makes everyone feel welcome."

Baltimore Jewish Times

"An instruction manual about how to do a good performance, it speaks to me. Very well written thoughtful stuff, fascinating."

Avraham Rosenblum, *The Diaspora Yeshiva band*

"What he has basically done is written a lab book of his experiences for people to use and share. It makes me wish I was a performer."

Nathan Sobel, *Accountant (Amazon review)*

It's so deep, informative, poetic, and entertaining! It's a masterpiece. After reading the book, I would definitely feel more confident to get on that stage!

Shani, *Pianist (Amazon review)*

"A source of new ideas and inspiration in how I can do an even better job. Highly recommended!"

I Cox, *President/CEO Wheeltug PLC (Amazon review)*

"Tried and true nerve calmers, and methods to keep your audience hooked and happy, this book is a must for anyone looking to start a career in music/performing.

Maddie Papesh, *(Amazon review)*

"The standard when it comes to camaraderie, and healthy artistic sharing."

Mesoud Benasuly, *Guitarist and bassist N.Y.*

"Bar sales are way up whenever Paul plays. A real presence with a quality style."

Andrew Hollett, *GM Corus Hotel Hyde Park*

"Check this guy out, it's a kiddush Hashem."

-Ben Shapiro, The Daily Wire (Twitter)

"Paul is a master songwriter, tying up lyrics and music together to create a unique and spiritual bond. His performance is filled with love and joy and fun."

-Art Lisker, Executive DirectorLisker Music Foundation (Google review)

LIFE IS GRAND, BABY!

Notes on performing (being in the song)

PAUL TOSHNER

First paperback edition April 2021

Published by
Concord Publishers
5 Bartlett Rd., Monsey NY 10952

Cover photograph by Rosa De La Losa

ISBN: 978-1-7366345-6-1

THANK YOU

Thank you for buying my book. I hope it will change your life and improve the lives of the people who listen to you, and that you go places and enrich anyone who might be melancholy with a song and a smile. The whole book in a phrase is: getting rid of all the things that get in the way of your head, and also heart, from being in the song, for your interpretation. In the end the value of inspiration is often underrated, perhaps because it comes with high risks. But you can reduce those risks, and that's the aim of this book, and how it came about for me—one *note on performing* at a time.

For Aviva

With love

CONTENTS

SAMPLER

Most platforms offer a teaser page, so I have copied a selection to the front. If you have my book in your hands, please skip forward to the foreword.

Playing a song is like in playing golf or shooting pool, if you take a somewhat "distance attachment" approach, you pot more frequently. All the better when combined with "a dose of judgement", and is best if you can simultaneously apply "care".

An artist in the room is responding to, and/or intertwined with, what's happening with the people in the room, there is an exchange taking place. Don't be put off because music was highjacked by the DJs, so of course, there is a greater need than ever for live music and musicians. I have seen all ages responding in the most loving ways as to suggest that people crave live music and musicians. The DJ is to the musician, like the photographer to the painter; limited and compromised as an artist.

Being an artist is being true to yourself in your

performance, however it suits you at the time. Entertaining is paying attention to people; giving to them, and caring about them.

This book is for the frontman, bandleader, or soloist. Someone who takes responsibility for the flow, pace, structure, material selection, engagement, and many dynamics relating to audience relationship. It addresses the need to be concerned with the way something is delivered as much as what and where it is being delivered.

I hope my range of experience can be useful to ease a path for performers to deliver meaningful material. To help people put their mind to what they really want to do. To marry the logistical side of performance with the art. If you want to exercise any authority, then natural talent only gets you so far; it doesn't take you all the way. You also won't get all things right all in one gig, but enclosed are helpful ideas to review from time to time.

DR KHOO

I had a slot playing on a beautiful Yamaha concert grand in the Westfield shopping centre, Shepherd's Bush London, in the Gucci/DKNY section. I wasn't paid at all by the centre but playing every Sunday I would pick up jobs like an engagement party out in Sussex at some country estate.

One day a gentleman came by and stood for a while with his wife as I played, then he asked me when I finished if I would go to his hotel, I assumed to meet with him at a hotel he was staying at in London's West End to discuss some one-off gig. But it was to *his* hotel, one of many he owned; he was Dr Tan Sri Khoo Kay Peng, a Malaysian businessman and chairman and major shareholder of Laura Ashley plc. as well as owning this hotel chain among other businesses.

I packed up my rig, got in the car and every two minutes my phone would ring with someone from his entourage asking if I was ok, if I knew the way etc. I arrived and his stretch Rolls Royce was at the door, and was told to park my van directly behind it. They opened the door for me, and standing at the door to meet me was the General Manager, Andrew Hollett, and a bunch of staff, all at attention. I was offered wine and chocolates as they welcomed me in.

I was then ushered downstairs to one of the hotel's restaurants "Bel Canto", an opera restaurant in the basement, where the "stars of tomorrow" from the London Opera school would serve your meal and every fifteen minutes break into song.

We sat and I played for two hours, me, the GM, Dr Khoo, his wife and an entourage of lawyers and bodyguards. He would sit beside me and try to join in on the piano at times and his touch was that of a sledgehammer, I had to encourage a perhaps more sensitive approach. Eventually I said, "okay so what's going on?" He switched into business mode and we sat at one of the big tables discussing a price for me to play three hours a night three nights a week (eventually it became four hours a night four nights a week, and for three years). Then Dr Khoo asked, "do we pay you more than Westfield?" I answered him honestly.

"Well, yes."

A CLEAR VIEW

Performance is a great place to learn about yourself because an audience can be both loving and unforgiving in a very truthful way. Even if the money is not so good, the payoff is still huge. Not only do you come out from under the cloud of whatever you are having a hard time with; willful blindness, rigidity, prejudices against you (*or ones you hold*)—but it also brings a strong natural drive to move forward in an accurate positive direction.

You also come into yourself in a very true sense, and all things around you that are true are recognised, including a capacity for compassion which becomes much more relative. You get a clear view of the world and surpass many problems created by a lack of expression.

But what is that switch that gets flicked, that caused you to become deeply creative and confident during and after a good gig? It is that you are no longer so self conscious. But why? It is because you opened up and have been expressed to a group of people, and accepted. This is not a small thing. And so thereafter the more deep-seated hang-ups simply disappear into some wiser context naturally. This is being happy with who you are and what you are. While they are still different, and one does not excuse the other, but like said they enhance each other if you strive for both.

Mental health can be a state of mind
Don't think me rude or worse unkind
I mean to say try not to be blind
With expression you can change
and a new perspective find
It's not a quiz, or an intricate game,
but safe never is
and doubt is the brother of shame

FRESHNESS

Success depends on taking responsibility for timing as well as speed. It's a fine balance. If you consider an idea too long prior to expression, you lose something necessary to make the communication effective. Your concentration has to be so that just one second before the word, you have to know what it means as well as the note. A rhapsody of melody and contemplative symphony.

It's the same reason that Marlon Brando preferred using an earpiece with lines fed to him, heard for the first time there and then; the freshness of a random song-pool makes for a similar greater connection to a piece.

PARTING THOUGHTS

"Playing the game is better than winning the game."
"Having an excuse may not be an excuse."
"Be modest, be happy."
"May your needs and wants find harmony in your will."
"There are easier and more difficult truths."

FOREWORD

With Mesoud on guitar

The foreword is written by my best touring buddy Mesoud Benasuly. It was a shock, but Mesoud helped me realize that I do something that makes me happy. He said most people don't get joy out of life. As usual, what a friend, and what an amazing thing to say.

Mesoud has invented me in many ways!

"I wish I'd have met Paul Toshner 30 years ago. He has taught me many things about the world... about work; gals; money; investment; how to deal with people under any circumstance; fairness, kindness; hard work; consistency; the value of perseverance; the importance and the guts to destroy your own work if necessary, in order to start up again from zero, just to upgrade that 'little' notch; the absolute always essential tool of not taking things too seriously, especially and more particularly oneself! The ability to make connections and keep them hot, the strength to admit one's own errors and the bravery to live as happily with them, and ultimately, the ability to look at the heavens and beyond, with both feet firmly established on the ground...I admire Paul Toshner, I feel honoured to be allowed to call him my friend.

Togetherness is very important in this world. It can be with a person or with a thing or both; for example, Paul's togetherness with music, singing and playing has allowed him and propelled him to withstand the tests of time. It's a higher degree of fusion with something.

In the world of G-d, the concept of exclusiveness doesn't exist. Everything is fused, everything works organically when G-d is looking at His world. In fact the higher kabbalists and sages and ascetics all agree: the world of G-d is all inclusive, absolute fusion, absolute togetherness. You can get to feel that when you are fused with, absolutely united with, your craft."

Mesoud Benasuly, Guitarist and Bassist N.Y.

PREFACE

WHY BABY TOSH

My father's friend used to call my father "Tosh", because our last name is Toshner. So I would go with my dad to this garage for "choir practice" on a Friday afternoon. For "choir practice" he'd pull his office drawer out and it had a bunch of booze in it. The fellow's name was Gordon Templeman and he would call my dad "Tosh", and I was just a wee boy and I'd go with him, and Gordon would say "there's baby Tosh".

Hi, nice to meet you.

I hope you are going to enjoy my book.

My name is Paul Toshner (aka baby Tosh), and the accident of gathering the ideas in this book is significant. This is my first ever book, and it wouldn't have come about were it not for a divine design of five elements coming together:

Earth, wind, water, fire,...and the 5th element.

1. EARTH: 25 years of entertaining.
2. WIND: Loosing a year of bookings because of Covid-19.
3. FIRE: 10 years of studying the Talmud (which gives you an organised mind).
4. WATER: Pausing to reflect on my trial-and-error notes and noticing the makings of a book.
5. The support of my wife, Tamar.

Within these pages, I share secrets and stories from my years as a concert act, country club act, piano shop recital room act/clinician, a lounge act, piano-bar act, a shopping-center act, a restaurant act, and a assisted living homes act. Modes of understanding both technically and spiritually. Added are some more personal mémoire-like moments and "lessons learned." Together, this is my humble offering to the world from experience, which I'm happy to share and hope will enhance your skill and expertise as a performer.

JUST BE HUMAN
A newer game.

In the beginning, I saw that music and performance and song could rise me up out of situations I was in (the not so good, the bad, and the ugly), and then I saw it could do that for other people too.

As well as a sense of belonging, live performance is one way to bring the confidence of reality onto the bumpy road of life. That's also what makes it seem so daunting to get into. Indeed performance gets out of you the stuff you want out, but it also puts in the stuff you want in. The goal is to not mask things but do something expressive as a channel to realise in a constructive as well as cathartic way.

The simplest advice people often give is "keep it fresh" (*a newer game*) or "just be yourself": both may well be right, but usually come without any mechanistic or platform insights to stand on. I hope my book brings a deep and practical understanding to these abstract ends, and that you recognise useful dynamics from my stories.

I have heard people of all ages complaining about, "How come such terrible music gets made these days? Why is that? And how come it gets bought?"

I say, "it's because there are two marketplaces out there. There's a market for it because there are people out there without a heart, and there are people out there with a heart."

But that's not entirely true; more true is there's a lot of people who keep their heart a secret. And sometimes it becomes a secret from themselves. I know of two ways to tell the truth; through performance and by studying the Talmud, but the newest thing is always marketing! So, if you don't like to be sold entertainment, you'd better not read this or you might get too near a climax of reality.

Most guys are shy, and it's a natural thing for a guy to be shy, where as what's inside most men, if they are not shy, but if they not arrogant, it's a very beautiful thing and music brings that out. Music gets to the heart of the very best of people. "If they say, Why (why?). Tell 'em that it's human nature," as the old Michael Jackson lyric goes.

It's the world within you that you bring out; it's the world without you that you're in.

Don't let the tensions and the pressures overwhelm you.
Our standards are bigger than this.
Fight for the right to determine the venue,
a place where meaning can exist.

Kicking and screaming is fine if they drag you,
to a world that is just the abyss.
Remember that value is never defined by vocation,
or season, or even a kiss.

Look for no more in yourself or others,
no greater complexity chimes.
No standard, or bearer of words or tunes,
however refined are the rhymes.

Seek to be seeking, live to live,
reactions and actions combined.
And remember triumph's a game!
Love is The Name!
May the best man win, or complain.

Chapter One

THE BEFORE

"I neither believe in mere labor being of avail without a rich vein of talent, nor in natural cleverness which is not educated."

Quintus Horatius Flaccus, 65–8 BC

"Just find a place to make your stand, and take it easy."

The Eagles

"Beauty begins the moment you decide to be yourself."

Coco Chanel

TIME MANAGEMENT

ON THE DAY, BEFORE A GIG

On the day of a performance, I either make sure I really don't have too much to do, whether I feel like it or not. This includes clearing out the hours after a performance to allow for choices at the time, including doing nothing. Or have my schedule very well understood and generously spaced. It's important to not feel rushed.

If you need a nap, take a half hour (no more), but avoid it if you can. If you need to practice, play for a half hour (no more), but avoid it if you can. The lack of pressure "in the living room" induces a false sense of confidence, or being particular in practice dulls the senses necessary for giving an audience attention. Pianists: if it's a cold day, run your hands under hot water for a minute. Singers: breathe in for 5 seconds and hold for 5 seconds, and out for 5 seconds, then the same again for 7 and 8 and 9 seconds and you are done. Or you can hold out your tongue with a cloth, pull it out a bit, and go through the vowels to the tune of 'The Star-Spangled

Banner'. I usually do a quick warmup (I use Jeff Rolka http://
www.jeffrolka.com) but if caught short will use the first 10
minutes of a gig as a warm up before I reach for anything
difficult to sing.

It's best not to have any rehearsal prior on the day of a gig,
but certainly on the day after the gig is great.

Don't don't don't eat within two hours of the
performance because of what is called a postprandial dip –
your body uses a lot of energy to digest food, plus you'll be
burping the way through. Also try to avoid headache pills 2–
3 hours before.

ON THE DAY, AFTER A GOOD GIG

This is when to make business calls, having been "well
connected" with people, you will connect with anyone. Also
recording, filming (especially without rehearsal), or rehearsal
are good to do at these times. In rehearsals it's best not to
allow boyfriends or girlfriends, husbands or wives of the
players.

PRICING

In the beginning, you have to meet other people in the same
game as you, and without fear of competition tell them what
you charge and ask what they charge. And then price
yourself honestly, which means if you feel you offer more
than the norm then make your price at the top end of what is
acceptable. If you feel you are not yet where they are, then go
in below the norm. It's good to remember, like school teachers

or any vocational work, the more satisfying your work, the larger the gaps may exist between quality and price.

BILLING

I used to do a three-hour show, that was a mistake. An hour and a half is the maximum. I prefer to be booked for an hour and do the extra half hour. It's a sort of an "everybody's happy" situation, and I can cut a concert short if it's not exceptional and not leave anybody too unhappy. I have always operated with a damage limitation mindset.

The more you work like that, the more you will understand this is how it works in "entertainment" and other business also. It's how you keep the audience happy, as well as the people who book you.

THE DAY AFTER A GOOD GIG

This is an ideal day for internal organization and the sequencing of events.

This is also a day to watch for addictions, be that eating, drugs, alcohol etc. It's always the next day or two they are likely to pop up because some excitement seems missing. You feel a dip, and that's when to be a bit more vigilant. Going up is easy. Nobody is afraid to go into space (to get hi). The metaphor is for when you go up in expression, it's the "coming down" to earth that can be difficult, because it's become so far away. It's helpful to notice the distance.

Regarding pace in general, I prefer a maximum of four concerts a week.

FOOD TO HAVE ON THE DAY

Fruit, chicken, fish, nuts, peanut butter, honey, warm water, and a shot of something (I like Tequila, but Brandy mixed with honey is softer on the voice).

FOOD TO AVOID ON THE DAY

Dairy, coffee (I understand this is not a reasonable request), anything spicy or sugary, chocolate, cold drinks, beer or wine.

CLOTHING

Have shoes or something you play in. You need to feel this is something different from the norm.

PRAYER FOR RAIN

Either that morning or when I arrive in the car I make a small prayer composed for me by a Dr Rabbi Jack Cohen.

"Thank you, G-d, for the opportunity to perform – to bring people warmth and to give them joy. With your mercy, give me the wherewithal and the passion and the electricity to perform with fire."

SLEEP

There is something about being shattered that makes for a great performance—odd as it may sound. So never let your tiredness worry you pre-gig. If it is in the extreme, then chatting a bit more with your audience can really help.

SHARED ENERGY

This brings me to the strangest thing in the world. Maybe there is something to really learn from it. If you put energy into something shared with other people ... you receive energy. If you put energy into something that is just for yourself, you get tired and wasted and wrecked and wiped out. The longer I get to know an audience, the more time I spend where I get a feeling that we're together – the more I can play (even if I arrive tired, upset, or heartbroken)!

RESPONSIBILITY AND FREEDOM

An audience is like one person, and that person is someone you can give to, and give and give again, and they will give more back to you. Like a talented giver in any relationship, e.g. husband to wife, or supplier to client, with performer and audience there is that same balance of obligation and allowance.

SETTING UP

Ask in advance for set-up time; you can say, "Sometimes I need an hour and a half access to the performance area, especially for the first time. It's okay if people are there. Once set up there is a 5 minutes max sound check for your unique room."

The breakdown should be about:
- rig set-up: 20 min
- sound and equipment test: 20 min
- meet with people: 20 min
- buffer 30 min (essential)

"Anyone who says he is not nervous before a performance is a liar."

Luciano Pavarotti 1935–2007

UNWANTED ATTENTION

While you're setting up, you may want to take some attention off yourself or relieve some uncomfortable staring by some bored people. If so, find something to stare at yourself, and for a good minute, they will start staring at that thing too – then go back to what you were doing.

BUT A GOLDEN RULE. When you first enter a room, even if you are two hours early, say hello to the people in the room. This will help avoid some of that boredom voyeurism.

Also, while setting up, pay attention to something someone may say that people laugh about – and see if you have a song that fits – or make one up that fits. Even do this while you set up, or wait till during the show.

SET UP & STAGE FRIGHT

My worst mistakes have always been because of dealing with some technical issue when I should have been available to the people in the room _{see last story in Chapter 5 "Giving in to win"}. It is a must to be set up and ready with nothing to do for at least half an hour prior to first entertaining. The negative chain-reaction of events spurred on by not keeping this rule can be catastrophic.

Regards honest mistakes made, make the mistakes honest. Which means covering up usually makes things worse.

One of the best ways to deal with a succession of bad

decisions; ie a song is not going well, you go on a tangent and that fails also, and again you don't "catch it". Take a break - go where the king goes alone. Put on some cool track while you are gone for 3mins. Then come back with some well known piece.

When setting up in a new venue, it's best to be understated – people like that, people relate to that. This means mostly keep your eyes down, which is always a good way to avoid distractions. It's a very great and brave thing you do, and you are giving people something precious, but this is one way to avoid attracting cynical flak prior to a performance, i.e. while setting up, or having just entered the building.

Setting up for a good performance is about removing fear; fear comes from all sorts of places, and usually when attention is distracted. A shot of Tequila to kill the awareness a bit can help, especially if there has been too long a gap between gigs (e.g. 2 weeks +). Sharing a song and your ability to technically get round the piece is mostly about removing the potential negatives that can get in the way. Talent is rarely the issue.

In some respects, the "exchange" or "the gig" starts the second you step out of the car onto the premises. Including setting up, your priority should be to the people that happen to be around. Be very polite and if there is something you have to get away to do, ask their permission.

If you have a regular gig, the staff become the priority over the audience. All in the name of avoiding things that can go wrong in that highly sought after and precious emotional landscape you are about to wage war in; never mind all the help and support they will want to give you. It's always a good idea at some point to sing: "don't forget to tip the waiter/waitress".

It's good to hum quietly to yourself as a vocal warm-up while you are setting up if you need it.

EQUIPMENT AND SYSTEMS

There is rarely a gig where I don't think, "oh there's another tweak in some area"; details that are always being honed. These are not as important as the more essentials, but it has been a research and development process through the years on:

• Set up process, equipment choices, software, rig design, props.

• Up-to-date song pool for quick visual reference.

• Best live blend entry/exit practices for tracks using *Anytune Pro+* on an iPad.

• Best live practices using *Ultimate Guitar Tab* app on an iPad or iPhone and a PDF of a personal chord book in *GoodReader* app, sometimes blended with *Anytune Pro+*.

• Spares bag: minimum (lean/no fat) essentials; from a wooden wedge to a small can of WD40, an all-weather jacket, underwear and a toothbrush.

• If there is a squeaky chair - bring in your own chair.

WHAT IS CONSIDERED READY

It is important to have a recognizable point in your setup process where you say loud and clear to yourself, "that's it, I'm ready". And then be able to switch out of the technical mindset. If you are early for the show, just play and stop as you feel. But know that you are ready to "go with the flow".

Chapter Two

REPERTOIRE

"Of things I'd rather keep in silence I must sing."

Comtessa Beatriz de Dia (c1140–c1200)

"The notes I handle no better than many pianists. But the pauses between the notes - ah, that is where the art resides!"

Artur Schnabel 1882 – 1951

"Don't play to the gallery. It's dangerous for an artist to fulfill other people's expectations, that's when they generally produce their worst work."

David Bowie 1947 – 2016

SONG POOL

One key (especially for singing) over and above technical aspects, is to sing about a subject you know. It's best if you have a "take" on a song, so then you can use your imagination to tell the tale - as it were. You don't have to know about it "at the time". You do have to have known or witnessed something similar in your life.

"You have to break your heart again and again to sing some songs. And with well known songs, the only thing you can bring to them is your entire life. A life that's been lived, the mistakes you've made, the hopes, the desires."

Bono 1960 –

Talent is being able to impersonate something real, having been something real, at the same time being able to live less self-aware.

There is another mode of singing, where the voice is treated more as an instrument of sound played against the rhythm in a creative way – ignoring the meaning altogether. This facility can and should be employed to varying degree.

The song that you think is going to be the good one, may not be, and the one you don't sometimes may be. So operating with a mix of desired songs to perform in a pool is a clever way to approach a set. Eventually, your song pool should make your show like a work of art in itself. One category into another category. Be sure of five artists you cover and offer by name to your audience; but passing around a song menu through the audience is a bad idea.

Also try to get "the accidental" into the songs themselves. This can be in the form of a chord or lyric departure, and is best done in songs you know best. This is for you to be as surprised as the people listening, so depart somewhere; as it interests you it interests them, drawing you both into a shared enjoyment.

There are entry points to bring your own songs into a set: setting up an original song with an explanation is a good thing to do, but sometimes just go into it without an introduction is also good i.e don't even say it's an original, go straight in. It's great to ask permission "would you mind if I sing one of my own songs?"

If I'm sad before a performance I play a sad song, but before people come in, I play it to myself. Because when people come you don't want to have such a sting in a song. This is something you will probably only understand by doing, but I don't recommend opening with the song you "reallllyyyyy" feel like. I do recommend knowing what that song is though and playing it a bit before people come in, but you will probably notice you just want to "go somewhere else". This also goes for if you feel happy or contemplative; find an appropriate song and dabble in it for yourself first.

Of course, as a set progresses you can hit on songs that fit your mood, and through that can for sure connect "that little bit more" with people, and then move on.

The key in much of this book is to facilitate natural forward movement during a performance. It may be counter intuitive but this means not planning in advance – i.e. no set written out.

The main trick is to understand your repertoire so that on the day and in the moment, you only think about what you are doing, not what you are doing so that you can get onto the next thing – to go with the flow you need to avoid chasing logic. What you should be doing is working expansively with the material at hand and staying in touch with your audience. This is "the spirit of progress" (momentum over leverage) as opposed to "the spirit of old" (leverage over momentum).

It's usually foolish and short-sighted to have pre-selected song choices. Avoid creating a set you "think" the situation requires, instead of the ones you just "want to try." It's still good to "give em what they want" – but this specific material for certain crowds should be done in a balanced way and approached in your own style.

PLAYING TO THE GALLERY

People may misinterpret what you've given them and express what they thought they saw/heard. Everyone has their own artistic imagination. There is nothing wrong in them doing so. But when they do it, to call that "success" is a little bit lacking. It's success in that they're listening to you. But have they understood what you intended to say? Not necessarily. But for you to buy into what they thought they heard is another form of "playing to the gallery", which everyone is guilty of at some point or another, but it's something to watch for.

Over the hours, days or weeks approaching a gig, slowly highlight some songs from your pool you would especially like to get to (if you can). Here is a little poem that perhaps illustrates the point.

I had a dream,
Or was it an idea.
They were both the same,
but had too much precision.
So I challenged my mind,
and I changed my vision,
and I came up with
a new decision.
I would forever try,
and the attempt would be,
the thing I share, with you as with me.
And the love increased, and pain did subside,
I recommend this when looking for a bride.
If the going's good,
no predicting what would,
it's living that's free
and that's not what you see,
when you plan too much,
when you're out of touch.
That's the story of truth,
Ah but how we still look for proof!

THE *GREAT* UN-KNOWN

It is best to somehow reach into the unknown at, or near, the beginning of a performance. It's not as important to know what you're doing. If you do things you know, you are always going to be okay, but your performance will inevitably be dull. Once you have gone past that first "reaching into the unknown" then you can get into the things you have had that extra confidence with in the past. Now able to approach them in a much fresher way as well. Connect with the piece, connect with the people—but connect with the piece primarily. To be in a state of flow is the kind of confidence you're aiming for, which is like throwing someone a ball and knowing they'll catch it.

THE SHOW MUST GO ON

There are times in life when you go through things that are particularly difficult; nobody gets away without this at various points. When this happens to you as a performer, it is important to stop trying to push forward and develop your art and your craft. *Now* can be the time to rest on the things you know well. Paradoxically it can be a great time for growth, just don't be hard on yourself.

FRESHNESS

Success depends on taking responsibility for timing as well as speed. It's a fine balance. If you consider an idea too long prior to expression, you lose something necessary to make the communication effective. Your concentration has to be so that just one second before the word, you have to know what it means as well as the note. A rhapsody of melody and contemplative symphony.

It's the same reason that Marlon Brando preferred using an earpiece with lines fed to him, heard for the first time there and then; the freshness of a random song-pool makes for a similar greater connection to a piece.

The best thing is when I hear how someone didn't know the words to a song, but they tell me they actually hear the words when I sing. This is my aim, to interpret lyrics to have meaning. The point is a singer must understand what the song is about—that's what gives the melody its strength, not the other way round.

REQUESTS YOU DON'T KNOW

First apologise, or play something by the same artist or on a similar theme. If you have nothing in the ballpark, then explain your repertoire metaphorically "If you ask the local Chinese chef to make you veal parmesan he will tell you to go to Luigi down the road, regardless that he is a chef and it is all ingredients anyway"; they will understand that it's better served in an Italian restaurant. I personally avoid certain artists. I may still like what they do but they're just not *my* thing.

You are justified when repeatedly asked by the same person to do something you said you do not know, to say, "I'll do it another time, not right now, I need to go and prepare."

Sometimes I shy away from overly popular songs, especially if I have done them many times. I think to myself, if I play that song, I won't do it well because people will be able to tell I've had enough of it – people can always tell. If you leave it alone for a wee while and then come back to it and give it a new spin, you can bring new life into it.

But you do have to make sure people can ask for something. The only time I sort of say no is when people are not specific and say, "Play songs we can sing along to", I will say, "There will be a couple of those, but mostly I do interpretive work on both well and lesser-known pieces".

MY SONG SHEET

Regarding my song sheet or Picketer app approach, they are perhaps uniquely specific to me. They are like a stabilizer. Sometimes I need it and sometimes I don't. The visual reference of the dotted lines are for things I often forget to do, so as to draw my eye as to what's there, and the bold letters are a shorthand. It's all about combining a trustworthy song pool and taking risks on pieces too.

The way I run a set has to balance going with the seat of your pants and having a structure. I have to be able to go with a whim, and commit to it, and deliver a structured show. It's done with signpost and options.

A show is running at it's best when I know that the choice for the next song comes during the tail end of the song I am in, just as I do the "pull out" from the piece. But you can not always have that intimacy flow, and so a structure of a kind needs exist as well.

"The best is always 70% preparation, 100% is guaranteed failure"

Alan Gestetner 1961 –

My ever-developing song pool chart / process

- **GR** means the app *Good Reader* the app where I have a PDF of chords blocks for songs gathered over the years. Which normally represents about 30% of the songs I play in a set
- **PV** is "Piano Vocal" by heart favorites
- **PTV - PV** is "Piano Vocal" into "Piano Track Vocal" using the *Anytune prop+* app
- **JCY** - are songs where the chords play well in a nice juicy way (originals and covers)
- The **SPOKEN** list are good narrative lyrics that work well as spoken poetry

THE PICKSTER APP

Find it in the app store; its icon is an upside-down blue hat.

This is a middle-road stabilizer for the selection process. You can always deviate when relaxed enough to trust your read on the crowd.

But it gets you to where you are comfortable thinking in a more operable sense according to the audience's needs. You are freer to make insightful decisions and more at ease.

As a beginner performer, you may fall out of the "flow" in your off-the-cuff song decisions and it's something you want to pay attention to and come back to.

Use the Picker app to randomly select song options. I have it set to show me two songs at a time. To be too concerned with the next song during a set is something that detracts from your attention to the piece you are currently in. In addition, having a set list is a lot of work and often must be reworked on the fly due to the needs of the room at the time. The Picker app is a happy medium.

I do, however, set up different "pools" of material for use in different types of gigs, and always have my fully original pool ready for when the gig allows for it.

For example, I have different "levels" of gig importance pools, where riskier songs are left out of the more important gigs (but not all of them; some risk in song selection is always necessary, and often where the best gigs start from).

This approach also prevents one of the cardinal sins of entertainment; that of having a pre-supposed idea of "aaaalllll" the things you want to cram into a show. It is more important to do less than a quarter of what you planned but with due attention.

YOUR "VOICE"

Repertoire selection is also something to do with what people call "finding your voice", not the voice in your throat, but in the way you play. What you love, they will love. But you have to love it. If I play a chord and I feel the notes are like a peach, a squeezy juicy gorgeous chord or note, even though it's a simple approach if I love it – they love it.

Finding the things that you love, the "way of it that you love," is not so simple, but worth establishing. Each piece should have something to do with the way you deeply feel about something in particular – whether that's a sound, or a type of literature, or even one line in the whole song.

VOICE MAINTENANCE

A singing teacher and voice therapy are different things. A singing teacher is good for exercising your range, a voice therapist is even better for understanding *your* voice.

On the morning of a performance, check if your voice seems ok. If not, have a little sing about four hours later.

When you get the chance, often in passing a boiled kettle, breathe in the steam. Try not to clear your throat with a cough, rather a swallow is better. Sip warm water at/before a gig. Burp. Hot tea and ginger.

I have heard these things are good for the voice, but I'm not really sure: a raw egg and pineapple juice.

FULL VOICE/BELLY SINGING

Belly singing need not mean Opera. It can be the chorus of 'My Way' or the end of 'Old Man River'. But you need a "Bel canto" song or two available for two reasons: 1) It creates a wonderful dynamic during the set before an "opening up" for a more sensitive piece. 2) If you can't keep the nerves off, a little operatic vocalization incorporates a sound that is assumed to be confidence as a part of its power. It takes the singing more off of your nervous system and onto your belly.

Note: If you are ever having trouble with your voice for the bel canto moments, you can let people know. Or open up for a soft open voice, more like a yawn, and you can get away with what would have been big notes until you get better. *Sorry if I made you yawn...*

I'm a baritone, so to sing tenor pieces I change the key. I always sit with a piece I love and painstakingly rewind again and again until I have the whole thing written phonetically exactly as I hear Pavarotti do it. I then know I'm approaching the words the best way possible before I start to embellish.

KEYS/TESSITURA*

How to identify keys is best done with a good singing teacher or with a lot of patience. You will have favorite keys; it's not just the "get the low notes and the high notes in" approach. Try to vary keys in your song pool, though it's okay to have favorites.

*Tessitura (texture): most acceptable and comfortable vocal range for a given singer; the range in which a given voice presents its best timbre.

YOUR FACE

At home or in the car make gradual in/out funny faces once a month, or as needed, for a minute. Your face should be moving about in slow motion representing different modes of inner feeling.

To be physically, emotionally, spiritually expansive = presence. In practice, this is to use the whole face and body to sing. This also establishes a "comfortable distance" as well as intimacy.

Try not to look in the mirror; it matters more what is going on inside you. The face exercise is to loosen any crystallized disposition hopefully into one more fluid.

There is too much emphasis on vocal perfection these days. You can sing off-key; it's okay. If you put your heart and mind into something, people don't care. Look at Bob Dylan.

And if the music doesn't sound just right yet, make some faces, you'll be fine!

Chapter Three

DURING (STAGE I)

TO ENTERTAIN

"An actor is at most a poet and at least an entertainer."

Marlon Brando (1924–2004)

"A man who works with his hands is a laborer; a man who works with his hands and his brain is a craftsman; a man who works with his hands and his brain and his heart is an artist."

Louis Nizer 1902–1994

"When people are having emotions from listening to the music, there is a certain satisfaction that comes from relating to a person as a human being. You can make yourself and other people feel good."

Billy Joel 1949–

ENGAGEMENT

ENTRANCE OPTIONS

THE INTIMATE APPROACH

I personally prefer being mingeling or on stage as people start arriving, playing a little and chatting a little. It's a throwback to the lounge years, but it also offers a warmer more intimate setting from earlier on.

And "don't waste your resources" in this situation can be a mistaken premise. If you have people there and you are entertaining, keep going. Play a bit pre-show and remember this is a great way for the show to start naturally. You don't need the element of surprise – *play*, vary it as you feel. I sometimes stop playing and choose a favorite jazz or movie track and go say hello or go to the loo.

But this approach is not always possible. Perhaps something or someone is on before you and you need:

THE "ENTRANCE" APPROACH

The hardest thing of all is simply walking over to your instrument – as yourself. Leaving it is easy. It's good to warm up a bit and strut a bit. As you come in, as you walk out to a performance situation, the first thing to do is glance around the room and make eye contact with your audience. A quick look in as many people's eyes as you can. It's a form of saying hello. Perhaps a dance to a short up-beat piece of music as you pull off a pair of gloves or take a jumper (*sweater*) off. Perhaps do it with an air handshake, or a small bow, or raise a glass in a toast, especially if it's a regular gig. Or develop your own signature thing. But overly programed moves can be just as bad as not being sure what to do. Your opening should in some way be a casual encounter. Just loosely in a shape. Vary it. It's a good idea, once the sound set up is done, to get away and mingle. But when you sit at the piano, commit and let your hands fall to create the tone and pace for how to progress a good portion of this first song. It can be good to start with some simple repetitive riff. I like best to do a build up jam, some loop piano thing, and make up a song a bit. But whatever you do, make it that bit less programmed of a thing at the outset.

DO NOT do the "half-half" thing – i.e. if someone is on before you and it is possible to sit at your instrument while *they* are still doing their thing – don't. Be away from the instrument prior to starting. This is to avoid nervous doodling even slightly. If you have not been in the room already, either entertain or get away from the performance spot.

If you are nervous then focus on being outwardly attentive instead of inwardly (on your own thinking). This kicks in your muscle memory, which in turn makes you less anxious. And within about ten seconds of the gig starting (as long as the sound is the way you want it), and you hear yourself out of the speakers, try to shift your perspective out of hearing yourself in your head to hearing "the room" (with you in it) - that really helps.

Its also very good to start a cappella before going into your first song when you are coming after someone else.

Being attentive at the start is important. If they want Billy, I do Billy. But I consider song openers like "dips" or "starters" before getting to the main course. It is helpful for engagement to cadenza as you start a first song, or to repeat select chords once you are into it, this is like doing an impressionist painting, and is a lot of fun.

With your best-known songs, it is important to treat them with the cadenza approach as you go through them at various intervals. This includes new chord progressions using the same lyric in certain places.

FIRST SONG

Excellence is "in the turn". To enter-tain; to enter and taint (to colour), to enter and part enlighten.

It's a good idea to make your opening song one you know well and so can make a new art of, and at the same time be able to comfortably look at your audience. But you can also be reading chords (but not the words), just as long as it's one you really enjoy. Or read your lyrics to chords you make up. The goal is individuality over technique. A good performance is when you feel like you are inventing on the spot.

It's great to create, you know you can wait,
or dive right in, taking an idea for a spin
Finding something new, reaching part of you
You and me that is, I mean!
Even the part that wants to scream
Thinking ahead – what will be said!?
Giving up fear – being right here

One is aiming to achieve the unconscious (or not too conscious) expression of self _{see telepathy story.} Paradoxically, you become far more conscious but also far more satisfied than normal.

It's hard to convey the exact point in time to implement this but regarding your opening (although it's good to have a plan), you must be fully prepared to drop it in favor of a natural sequence of events.

I recommend not choosing your first song (hitting the "pick" button) until after you are set up, and as close to the official start time as possible. And sometimes even not till you "play" the piano a bit randomly first. The best rule for an opening song, to paraphrase Albert Einstein, is "keep it simple but not too simple."

Also for a first song check what you are about to say in the opening lyric e.g. "While My Guitar Gently Weeps" is a bad first song because the first words are a direct criticism.

TALENT IN KIND

To give and receive a bit of kindness as well as talent, that's entertainment. This requires a balance of objective (impartial and factual) as well as subjective (personal) understanding in any piece. The goal is to be able to dedicate a part of every song as a "present" of its meaning to whomever is really listening. You may not be able to notice, but they are there and they want you to really "give" it to them, and when you notice them, let them know you appreciate it; not easily done while maintaining the focus required, but possible with your eyes.

It is worth noting that even the slightest joke at these serious moments can ruin the whole thing just as much as dropping focus.

Fairly early on you want to have covered two or three varied things in your style, approach, and song pallet, including:

- playing with the music in well known pieces, i.e. make the odd cadenza* to loosen things up before you start a song. Or on every chord of the song once you are in it, like an impressionist painting - repeating chords of the song as you feel, it's a lot of fun.
- looping is a good option because it layers your objectivity as well as being fun. (I use the RC300 loop pedal), see below**
- speak to them (perhaps recite a lyric as poetry without your instrument - even as the songs intro).
- a good thing to do early on, is find a couple of people in the audience to take note of who you can refer back to e.g. ask their name or favorite

food, perhaps someone has the same name as
your first girlfriend.

- look at the audience.

In total to cover two or three varied things quite soon.

* a chord departure or improvised passage played or sung in a "free" style, a parenthetical flourish.

- **LOOPING songs heavy on lyrics but limited
  in chord movement are ideal opportunities to get
  a loop going. You can also get away from the
  instrument and create a more expansive or
  juxtaposed delivery in the vocal.
- don't be afraid to leave the odd empty bar in
  creating the loop; it makes for a beautiful space to
  solo, fill, or link in.

In short, to risk intimacy as a performing artist, you must
flex some muscles near the start:

1: AN ATRY VOCAL

To sing "off the beat" creatively, adhering to your
understanding of the lyric. This is easier in a simple four-
chord song, which you can loop to free up any difficult
syncopation that comes to you, e.g. "He's Misstra Know It
All".

2: A POWERFUL VOCAL

Opera or some bel canto singing on a line, e.g. "My Way".

3: THE PHYSICAL

Either during a band/track assisted song where you can

get away from the piano or on a loop. Go closer to the crowd —just you, the microphone, and them. Lean and look at them.

The greater risk is to "stay in your shell" for too long. The more time passes where you don't break out with one or all of these, the harder things become.

GENERAL TALKING TO AN AUDIENCE

Slow down at the start. Later on, especially after a heavily lyrical piece, like a Bob Dylan song, speeding up your speech is no problem.

Share stories about what's happening in your life at that time. Whatever happened within a couple of days is of significance. Let them know, even if it was a colonoscopy; what's important is that you share your life. Oversharing is a matter of context; the better the gig, the more natural it is to share.

You are doing for them what you are doing to yourself, becoming liberated enough to be generous.

It's important to never reference your private intimate relationship, with your most significant other as a reference point for "the crowd" when entertaining – it's a false economy – it's not something that should guide your understanding. Unless you really have the kind or relationship where your partner is both a new girlfriend, as well as an old lover. You've got to read and feed, and feed and read the crowd. Like in all things it is from heartfelt giving, you get back the sweetest energy of life.

WHAT MAKES A GREAT PERFORMANCE?

It is when the connection between you and the people is deeper, and at the same time, natural. It sounds so simple! A great show is where it feels like you are talking to a friend— and now and then playing a song. That the song is somehow part of the conversation. Not that you are playing and *then* do a bit of talking. The emphasis should be on being with them. Chatting. Even though the amount of chatting you do may be less than the singing / playing.

The following is important to consider in a quiet moment on your own. As an entertainer, your job is in part to actually be there to give people the deepest parts of your attention – that which we all don't feel we get enough of in life. How is that achieved? Through the great lyrics and songs that you selectively perform. They are indeed the conversations we all long for. Talking to a good friend or going to a therapist is a similar thing. We all sometimes feel we need to share deep and trusted ideas on matters close to our hearts.

Some practical applications of that are:

Don't worry about being seen as trying to gain approval. This is part of the performance process and not a bad thing.

Talking more comfortably after a first song is a bit easier, rather than before.

I should mention it's not that you need other people to "tell you". You don't need to see yourself "outside of yourself" to know who you are or "where" you are. As I perform, I am happily taken by surprise by people loving what I do as I "expand internally". In getting to that place, I realise I am servicing a need. In some way, we all need a representative now and then. As an entertainer, you have done a great service. The most profound thing you can give someone you love is probably some subtle message found only in song. This is because each of us has so much to say that gets left unsaid! There's nothing wrong with you if you've got a lot that isn't said; because, when is the time to say it? Many emotions are buried, and you need the right medicine; every gig, every day, the different people — it's always a new combination. Every gig is a venture into a common space not yet revealed, and we are looking for the energy and the inspiration that will only be defined when you get there; it is then that your emotions will connect to that inspiration. This is the "pit stop" or the essential place to go; a necessary spiritual or religious exercise. So, what you do as an entertainer can be an important public service. You will enhance your ability to do this if, in your personal life, you also strive beyond duplicity. Then you are freer "to say the things you truly feel". The most realistic way to practice this is in quietly appealing to G-d, trusting He is bigger than what you perceive any problem to be. As a believer or not, for a moment, you can suspend reality to mimic this (the same as you allow for most movies).

I guess there's a need to simplify. Sometimes that means to detach from that which complicates. And their's a need to love. But if you're not up to the strength of character that it requires to *be* loved, how can you hope to love!

Being a bit cool with the audience is good too. It's a balance (not ignoring but to let them be cool with you too).

To help achieve this, sometimes imagine performing in a sort of a haze.

If you sit cross-legged at the piano with your legs more at

your side, it inspires the look and feel of being comfortable, which is what you want. And it should be exaggerated a bit, too!

My buddy Mesoud always makes me think – on one such occasion he made me consider the following. "Good. Why do you think a particular performance was good?"

It is when I connected with the piece, and I could see I connected with the people. That's my definition of good.

As if I am painting, where I connect with myself, but a group of people connects with it too, at the same time. Getting past the realm of the political to something shared "unpurchased", as it were, it's an achievement. And a shared achievement. In a world of compromise, we have a need for something less so. Our perception of G-dliness is one free of Earthly prejudices. Something G-dly happens when we do whatever art we do and find it sincerely accepted. To know something came up from the depths – in some personal context. We always feel when that acceptance is deep or sincere for two reasons. When we recognise quality and then simultaneously feel acceptance. There are always those who do not let their feelings show, but there are also those who do.

TRICKS OF THE TRADE

The more you have something to speak to the audience about, that's related to the song; in those speaking moments, it's another similar type of "pit stop" which totally enhances the opportunity to want to give of the art. In short: the more you speak to them the better you play. Caveat: This is council for people who normally have their head down in the art of the song, and don't look up. This is not for the person who stands, and speaks, and chats away and doesn't pay any attention to the fact that they have over spoken, thats not who this is for.

You can also listen out for something said by someone in the audience, it can tip you off to a song you can pool from in your repertoire, something that addresses or has that point in it – that's the best way to choose a song. Be that at the start of the show or as it is running. But in balance with innovative approaches to songs you randomly choose. It is a good way to kickstart a creative performance. But it is mainly to avoid getting lazy and relying on songs you know you did well at other times – they invariably don't go well. This way, you will, in some way, develop your own art form.

If you do fall into that trap, or drift into average playing, a way out is to use what my wife calls "pallet cleansers."

I use some pieces as a sort of reset – "Zorba the Greek," "The Entertainer," "Piano Man."

EYE CONTACT

Don't take too long to look up, but avoid staring people down. Give individuals an even amount of attention. It's surprising how far you can see when it comes to people's eyes. When you notice someone giving you that "open to you" gaze you can look a little longer/give a little more next time round the room.

It's good to remember audiences and bookers are very loyal to regular performers. If you are the new guy, even if you are the best ever, and you've been in a few times but there is a long-time regular, they are still loyal to him – don't forget it!

SONG ENDINGS

Stop short of the last note/chord/beat.

Or make the emphasis on the upbeat on what would have been the last beat.

Or fade into almost nothing.

Or make sure in a few songs to segue into the next song; it's a nice balance that each song is not requiring of applause.

Or take the chords out of the key of the song for a second and come back for the last chord.

When you know that the people were really close and were with you all the way in a song, when you deeply feel and know that was the case, it's important to note that they are especially waiting for a signal to the end of the song, beyond the last note played. And at these times that can be more subtle.

Rehearsal situations should always be approached aware that the live ingredient is missing. Remember not to be offended when the mood seems to not reflect the sincerity you feel you can invest. For that matter in a live situation there are limitations relative to the freedoms allowed, as alluded to in the next section.

INTIMATE SONG

For some pieces that are extremely profound or intimate you sort of take a step back to inside the song, as if you were inside a room two feet away from a round window looking out at a beautiful view. You are just not right up against the glass. In that way people are looking further into you, and from there you can deliver stronger and more genuine emotion.

PHASES AND APPLAUSE

AUDIENCE TYPES

Most of this guide is for the concert performer, but the differences in the environments listed below can help explore what it means to operate within "given" limitations. Different settings enhance or limit how much you can expand. The situations below help demonstrate a necessary varying balance of courage and tact.

THE LOWEST:

RESTAURANT

Here people already have their entertainment in two forms: the company they are eating with and the food.

"Music with dinner is an insult both to the cook and the composer."

- Gilbert K Chesterton (1874–1936)

Or the company and the musician. This kind of gig is perfect to work on your instrumental repertoire, but you have to refrain from too expanded a dynamic because no matter how good you are, you are not why they are there.

THE MIDDLE:

LOUNGE/PIANO BAR

This is a level up. Here people can choose to come close to you, and so the level of dynamic and intimacy is vastly improved over a restaurant. However, there is still a glass celling to that magical space where you expand and reach the corners of the room, be that a concert hall, a stadium or an assisted-living facility (where you are engaged to perform a show).

THE TOP *WHERE THERE'S ALWAYS ROOM...*

CONCERT

This is the best. Here you are only limited by factors relating to your own performance. Here you can not only reach into the corners of the room, as if everyone is seated right next to you, but you can reach into corners of yourself that you never knew were there. If a large audience seems like a monster and you are more comfortable with smaller intimate settings. Dealing with a larger room, look at the people closest to you as the head of the dragon, and the people at the back the tail. It's the head that wags the tail. To do what you do with a few, with many.

THE BEST AUDIENCE

The development of a concert is always going up in levels as the show progresses, this is easier with a more expressive audience (eg USA is less reserved than UK). For a more reserved audience you must do more wild things to get them going. The best audience is always an expressive audience. But they must also have their privacy. If you can't turn the lights down on them then you need to make sure not to stare anyone down. But you still need to be able to see them a bit.

APPLAUSE

It's a funny thing, if you really want to know how much an audience appreciates a performance you gave, it's in the sound of the silence just before the applause. The greatest success is being able to whisper a lyric at some point.

In the above settings, apart from where you are booked as a concert act, you can get away with a "substandard" performance. As a concert act, you can't. The demands are greater but the satisfaction and room to expand is broader. Everyone is better suited to being a concert act, but doing some time in the other arenas can be helpful if you feel you are not up to it yet.

I once had my best performance ever in a Hilton piano bar. The room was packed but I was applauded perhaps only twice in a three-hour gig. I didn't know why that was when something great really took over, but the setting meant the music was taken for granted as background. It was very dark as well. It took me a bit of time to realise when I left that was why I only got applause a couple of times.

Whereas in a concert setting, the first, or sometimes a very heartfelt applause, can leave you wondering – what on Earth do I do here now?

But after getting that first/or sincere applause – relax, chat (slowly) – you're in!

E.G.:

- "I love to sing this next song."
- *Or:* "It's a great song."
- *Or:* "That was / this is for you" directed to one person.
- *Or:* Explain what you did or are about to do.
- *Or:* Ask permission: "can I take my jacket off?"
- *Or:* Tell people about the song /some background info.
- *Or:* Tell people who wrote the song / abut them.
- *Or:* Let them know if it is someone's favorite.
- *Or:* Tell them a "secret / private" story.

PRESSURES

"If I tell you I'm good, probably you will say I'm boasting. But if I tell you I'm not good, you'll know I'm lying."

Bruce Lee when asked if he thought he was any good, 1940–1973

"Public pressure is like air pressure, at 14 pounds per square inch, you can't see it but it's there."

anon

"Sometimes when people don't know what you've gone through they can mistake your confidence for arrogance."

50 Cent, 1975–

There is something fabulous about being able to lean into yourself more as a performance progresses and find that untapped glorious stuff. As well as relating to an audience, this makes the music infinitely better. These phases can fluctuate and you can even hit a patch where you feel bored (shhhh!): but this is a good indication that you have to take some bigger risks, or choose more meaningful songs. Remember that you and your audience only have a limited time to get to know each other.

DRUGS

I don't have much experience with drugs but I can tell you what being on steroids (for a vocal chord condition) made me notice.

All concerts are a type of socialising, and it takes until 3/4 of the way through to get to the mode of performance where I know I'm doing both a service to the song but also reaching individuals more impactfully at the same time. But being on steroids I came in thinking I had it all going for me from the start, but in fact, it compromised the reality. I imagine other drugs also remove that opportunity for real connection.

LEANING OFF

Even though the act before you was good and the audience is excited for what's coming next, sometimes going on after a great act can make you feel intimidated. Regardless, no one in the world is as good at being you, and it's impossible that anyone is better at it. They may seem better at being themselves in that moment if they caught that "leaning" wind. However, this can be a good thing if you can lean off of that, if you can borrow from their feeling rather than rely on your own confidence. It's not necessary to play what they played (though that could work if you knew the piece) but something you know approached "in the style of" (with a similar feeling) or "on the subject of". That is "leaning off", and there is always something universal about that space where people are being themselves. Instead of perceiving a threat, you can see it momentarily as part of you. But don't forget this is so that you can transition with them. Be they laughing or crying, you still want to get them to where your approach and content is; this is just about making the transition less abrupt. It can be just a word, an idea, or a gesture. So if you are nervous, bring something of theirs into your approach. It's the same principle as a segue for a joke leading off of the last guy that comedians do. Of course if you don't need to do this it's better not to.

UNWANTED QUESTIONS

Some questions are because people are interested in the answer; some are just because they want to be questioning, perhaps to suggest some vulnerability. The better you are, the more humble you can be. Not meek, but humble. And if you cannot reconcile being good at what you do and being humble, perhaps you are neither – one is always part of the other. But if you ever sense that type of pressure, usually it alludes to being limited or defined, it's best to reply with "I do what I do", and it's still treating it professionally to reference it as "work but fun", or "I love it." As things get more and more real, you forget more and more about yourself or taking things personally. No one is perfect, but it's your ability to live through or "past" yourself that's important. It's always better to feel like you have gained respect than to receive compliments – it means more, though compliments are good, too ;).

"Nobody's jealous of a man without ambition."

Mesoud Benasuly

PRIVATE COMPLIMENTS

If people come up to you after and tell you they were moved to tears. Don't tell them, e.g., "It's good to have a cry". You are not suddenly in a position of authority in their life. Either nod and say nothing, or if you can get away with it, say something light like "oh no!" in a slightly whimsical way. But however sincere, much more of a response is not appropriate.

At these times, it is important when you say "thank you", say it quietly so only the person who gave you the compliment or who opened up to you can hear it.

When complimented a lot - just say thank you - don't capitalize on it – that is the key – hard when things have been a struggle, but it's what you've got to do. Don't try so hard.

CRITICISM

If someone directly criticizes you, you can reply with a simple, friendly, and disarming, "Ah, I see you really want to be my friend... I understand!"

REFERRAL

It is important to try not to take jobs only upon referral. It's hard to resist, but it's better where you either auditioned, chased the job, or were seen playing by someone. In these instances you will have naturally established a relationship with the people you are going to work for. The same way when someone recommends someone to you there is always that slightly awkward dynamic in the relationship. It's a compromise, and one that is more costly in the arts. The best thing you can do is find someone you have your own rapport with. Even if you find someone who is meant to be "the very best" if the rapport is not good you will end up with less than with someone less touted but the rapport is good (it need not be perfect, but good is great.)

"The way to the top is always from the bottom."

A GOOD WORKMAN *CAN* BLAME HIS TOOLS

It is of paramount importance to play a real piano. If you can't afford it and you have to take a job with a keyboard, it happens. It makes a big difference though. I never get the feeling of, "oh, that was a tough room," when I had a real piano to play. Literally, it is a tool to make a better connection.

If an outcome is either exciting enough or some significant problem avoided, then the risk is worthwhile. Below is a communication I sent when I started to try yo keep to this decision:

Hi

Thank G-d I'm getting more bookings as Covid looks to be clearing up, and combined with how much I love a real piano, and how much I feel at a loss with a keyboard, I have decided, at the moment, to only do piano gigs.

I'm not being a stick in the mud. I just love a real piano and it makes a difference to what I can offer, as well as I find keyboards so lacking.

It's a difficult decision because, of course, I need the work. But as you offer both I have decided I'm only available for the bookings on a real piano.

I hope you understand.

Best

Paul

That said, I must be honest I fluctuate between not minding keyboards because I enjoy the crowd. But it's an illusion. On a grand piano, the radical difference in performance is huge. On a keyboard, you can control the sound much better for looping, and you don't get sticky notes either. But the sound and so performance quality is that much better on a real piano.

The following insight was gathered just after performing for an older New York crowd—I don't think you will get a tougher crowd. And to my surprise, the venue had a keyboard and no real piano.

If you ever find the need to get through a really tough

room then letting out your frustration early on in a managed way is an approach. You may know it's not your fault, but it can still be difficult. And there are many things you wish you could say. But you start to run ahead of yourself so that you don't think; you run away from your thoughts and you do it on purpose. And you see thoughts coming that would talk you into some response, but you speed up, including your playing, so that they don't catch up. In this situation you can let out the frustration a bit in the lyrics or sneak it out in your performance. Just to take the sting out of *you* a wee bit, but then dial it back, and you will find you will be okay.

You also have to push them a wee bit to participate. If you stay too quiet they will roll over you (i.e. not engaging /not talking directly and pushing for a response, which with a better crowd you don't have to think about).

BE PREPARED, AND WORK WITH A TEAM.

The ones who are overly nice when booking you are often the ones who end up telling you what songs to play. Never buy into anyone's praises before you start. Also keep in mind a good performance will still have people who want to exercise their personality, and you will overhear something like, "ah, he's just rehearsing!" But you will also have people who will come up to you and speak earnestly—don't worry, it's them not you! I once had two people at the piano at the same time; one complimenting and the other berating.

Be prepared for comments from "the know-it-alls." They may even be good musicians but be prepared for them. You need to be a bit firmer and, feed them back in your own words, in complete agreement with whatever they just told you. Even better ask them to flat-out agree back with you.

The longer you talk to cynical people, the more they feel they have something "to work with." But you can relax because the more people are cynical, the more they don't do things only really understood by doing. People who are solid with substance are too focused on brass tacks (purpose) or some hard intellectual problem.

Again: "Be modest, be happy."

To be specialized requires working with other specialists.

Is it about the song? Or is it about you? Discuss...

The answer is: both. But in what measure and why!?

Any kind of art is so enjoyable because you can get lost totally in it – and totally found! Regarding my best work as an artist, I feel the same way, and yet ... there is always an operational mind driving forwards with a push and pull. Dancing a little too close to edge, it may seem. But still, as a halfway decent artist, you are intrinsically driven to be deeply involved with many a great truth. So, you sort of have to make your mind up:

Which pain do you prefer? Hating yourself for living a lie – and so compromised in your work? Or being hated by others for not living with *their* lie – and so being exceptional in your area, but losing out on some bookings?

One of the hardest things is dealing with effusive praise leading to promises at the end of a gig. This is why you really need a team, a person to talk money, another to talk detail, another to talk delivery. I have been thrown under the bus, where in the end the booker traded "their word for their job" – at least that's how they saw it.

You know how to navigate
the seas that are rough,
the trail that blazes
you've got that stuff!

Maintaining a connection
hi or low
coz you're in the middle
wherever you go.

Quoted yes you are,
but understood so very little
sometimes devoid of that...
of a world,
that's become so brittle.

DEALING WITH THAT ONE PERSON IN THE AUDIENCE WHO WANTS TO DERAIL THE SHOW DURING THE SHOW

When this happens, it's an internal, not external, battle. This can also be in the form of someone rapturing about how fantastic you are, when everyone else is being politely quiet. You have to nod to them like you nod to everyone else to give them a sense of what a normal state of mutual respect is.

If one or two people are talking over your performance, but the rest of the room is quiet, usually other audience members will take care of it for you. The situation will probably pass. Focus on the folk enjoying the show to let it go. Then do what you can to make them love themselves, that's the only thing that really works. But if it escalates, you may have to stand up in a controlled but more firm way—as with all things in life. For example, if someone's phone keeps ringing, it's challenging, but best dealt with by using a little humor. After three or four times, say, "seven is my limit, then we do a test to see if it will still ring in my glass of water", or "we've got a dial in audience these days, everybody get your friends to phone in and hold your phone up".

> "There are four types of temperaments. One who is quick to become angry and quick to calm down — his gain is outweighed by his loss. One who is slow to become angry and slow to calm down — his loss is outweighed by his gain. One who is slow to become angry and quick to calm down is pious. One who is quick to become angry and slow to calm down is wicked."
>
> Pirkei Avot (ethics of the fathers)

During a multitude of conversations coming at once you need to talk over whatever subject you choose to ignore - people will move with you. You don't need to "deny" someone their subject, just stay on track and the head of the beast will change with you.

It is always true, in your deepest moments of inner turmoil, if you manage to calm yourself, you will discover the greatest things.

Restraint:
The secret to sacrifice
Sacrifice:
The secret to understanding
Understanding:
The secret to gratitude
Gratitude:
The secret to restraint

GOOD DECISIONS

Success makes people make good decisions because they have the confidence to exercise them, and with commitment. This is because it was some sort of commitment, and deferred gratification, that brought them to that success, instead of a half-baked decision that kept them going in circles.

When I do well in a gig, I know what my decisions should be in other areas too. However, I still sometimes let them slip out of the fear of knowing that "I'm not always on that level".

And so good decisions should be made after good decisions; likewise, bad decisions you should try not to make after bad. Ultimately, it is wisdom to commit to good decisions made in a good place.

"A moment's thought can save a year's labor."

Ivor Tiefinbrun MBE

COMPLIMENTS GRACIOUSLY ACCEPTED

"We try our best" is good,

or "it's good to share",

but "Thank you" is best.

And do not underestimate the incredible impact you can have after a good gig, when the best thing you can say to your audience is "thanks for giving of yourself in the way that you listened".

BEING A PIRATE

"Maybe" is to ponder
A place the mind can wander
It may even be fun
But best still bring a gun

Coz know you do not, whatever you've got
Whatever you get, lest you regret

So again I shall say
A gun is the way
To shoot down those doubts
Wherever their shouts

And stand in your pain
With your head all the same

As such in the clouds
But above the rain

Where the fight can begin
The only one we can win
The one called commitment
At least until the next shipment ;)

Yes pirates we are
Stealing harts for their joy
Stealing time in their smile
And we'll set sail in a while

And our bounty will be
Just to be you and me
To sing our drunk song
And leave them singing along

I toast you my friend
Without whom the road would not bend
And while the sky it may weep
Still we serenade him to sleep

So fight on I do say
With tears in our eyes
With grit in your soul
If you're half less than whole

All be it for one moment, and in a brave mans death
Be hearty my mateys, as yet we've not left.....

McDonald's *Brent Cross*

Joining in at **The Crystal** *St Moritz*

The Danubious *Regents Park*

The Danubious *Regents Park*

The Chesa Grischuna *Klosters*

Café des Art's *with the Davidoff trio Basel*

With Tara Palmer Tomkinson in Klosters. During the season people would also ask you come play at private functions in their chalet.

Brightview *Assisted Living, east coast USA*

50+ centre *Ellicott City, Baltimore*

Fountainview *Monsey, New York*

Princess Square, *Glasgow*

zur Alten Brauerei, *Celerina*

Westfield shopping centre, *Shepherd's Bush,
London. With Dr Khoo, his wife, lawyer and bodyguards,
as he picked me up for what would be a three year stint at
his Corus hotel Hyde Park.*

Sinatra Sundays *Corus hotel Hyde Park*

At the Corus

At the Corus

At the Corus

At the Corus

At the Corus

On the way to his OBE from the Corus

Pre RAF dinner at the Corus

Photograph by Rosa De La Losa at the Corus

Photograph by Rosa De La Losa at the Corus

Photograph by Rosa De La Losa at the Corus

Photograph by Rosa De La Losa at the Corus

Photograph by Rosa De La Losa at the Corus

With Mesoud on guitar

With Mesoud on guitar

With Mesoud on guitar

With Mesoud at The Albert Hall

Rolling Hills, Baltimore

Shelton, Connecticut

Toms River, New Jersy

Wellspring, Baltimore

Bastille Taverne *Glasgow with Rich on drums*

At the Aviemore Coylumbridge Hotel Scotland

The Rig

The set up

Chapter Four

DURING (STAGE II)

THE MUSE

This book, like a show, goes through phases as it progresses; **Chapter Three** STAGE I (to entertain) was dedicated to making a connection. Now **Chapter Four** STAGE II (the muse) is about navigating that world of greater intimacy.

"To laugh often and much; to win the respect of intelligent people and the affection of children; to earn the appreciation of honest critics and endure the betrayal of false friends; to appreciate beauty; to find beauty in others; to leave the world a bit better whether by a child, a garden patch, or a redeemed social condition; to know that one life has breathed easier because you lived here. This is to have succeeded."

Ralph Waldo Emerson 1803–1882

"Do I trust the audience!? Yes of course, Pavarotti could not be Pavarotti if he did not."

Luciano Pavarotti 1935–2007

"If you are not doing what you love, you are wasting your time."

Billy Joel 1949–

"A man has to serve his talent, but not at the cost of his principles."

Mesoud Benasuly 1972–

SPIRITUAL

FIRST: AT YOUR DEPTH

Becoming the artist you are is intertwined with the person you are. Any idiot can be a genius. The most satisfying work in life is character, most truly. It's hate that will ultimately erode determination. Meaning the drive toward any aspiration will suffer as a result.

"Hatred; the coward's revenge for being intimidated"

George Bernard Shaw 1856–1950

And so it follows that love is the brave mans reward for being courageous.

Great music has less to do with how you can play or what you can do than with who you are (which, in turn, is influenced by what you are). What and who you are go together, but one doesn't supersede the other. They are different. I hope that's not too complicated. What you are is the raw material, or that which needs to be uncovered, learned about, and understood.

Who you are is what is seen by how you express yourself. Who you are is what this book is about, but *what* you are has a profound effect on developing that *who* part. One more intrinsic but bolstered and revealed through the practice of the other. One, the engine room where you derive comfort, direction, and inspiration. The other, the captain's deck.

There are many ramifications to this. For me the "what you are" is Judaism. Although I agree you that can't look to something to know things for you, you have to understand things for yourself. But that's what studying Gemara (*the component of the Talmud comprising rabbinical analysis, studied exhaustively generation after generation—the science of Judaism*) helps you do. But it can be any lifestyle choice you see as inspirational and deeply relevant. The following is an introduction to my feelings about the study of the Gemara.

MY "OBSERVANCE"

I usually have more in common with a religious non Jew than an irreligious Jew. Although I have never met a Jew without G-d. They are either for Him or against, but never without; deep down I find little apathy on the subject. Israelis come up to me after a gig when they discover I'm observant and say incredulously, "You are religious! But you have everything, why do need that, there's nothing wrong with you!" and I answer that before being observant, music was "a jump", something "used" to "come up"; now it's more of "a fall", something you can "let drop", and I enjoy it way more than ever. In short, to give out what is in you. Instead of reaching to music for spirituality, you have it to give. Music is still a

wonderfully truthful vantage point. But not everything it pro
ports to be.

All my structuring skills from equipment, to performance
approaches, to the form this book has taken, would never
have been possible were it not for the study of Gemara for the
last sixteen years. It is there that the capacity for abstract
thought in a framework is exercised.

I learn every morning before getting into my daily
routine. I am on my fifth Masechta (*a tractate, an
organizational element of Talmudic literature that
systematically examines a subject*) with a chavrusa (*a learning
partner*) of twelve years –Tuli Dubiner of Sassov, Golders
Green London, as well as another Masechta with Eli
Gestetner in New York.

An invitation to share in the Gemara with someone is to
share in truth, to share in perfection, to share in real
happiness. I have never enjoyed being wrong so much. Like
children have less hangups about being wrong, and are
therefore continually creative, it keeps you young. It is the
ultimate in "the golden middle road," and so affords the
greatest dynamic potential – it is a wonderful conversation to
be part of! And a most essential exercise for people who feel
they are, as yet, in a situation where they can not risk "real"
dialogue.

"There is no hype around the Gemora. You just have to do it
to know what's fun or geschmack (flavorful) about it. There's no
real good way to sales pitch learning. You just learn it and
when you get it, when you feel it, it's powerful and it's there,
but it's abstract. It's logic, it's a whole world that's not
explainable. If you are not in that world there is nothing to

say. You have to just do it and you will see what it has to offer. And that's a very hard nisayon (trial) for a lot of people, bocherim (young men) today especially. Because sadly the "You learn, wow!" has been lost in a certain way. There is no bo-lishma (do it for the wrong reason to come to the right) any more, to start you off with a connection to the Torah, no superficial kovod (honour) in it"

Moshe Siegal, *music producer*

All said; I see the Gemara and all of Torah as a fine wine you can savour; the ingestion of which appeals and relates to something wonderful and refined. Even my father, a staunch atheist, said twice after the few times we learned: "it's amazing; you feel really good about yourself after it."

The same way you let good music in without questioning what you allow to move you from one place to the next, to take you on a journey, to feel now, and then at the next, that takes you somewhere else, Gemara is the same but so much more. It strikes with the same profundity as Puccini's "Nessun Dorma" sung by Luciano Pavarotti, in my opinion the greatest singer, singing a piece of such humanity, such nobility, melody and content. All our souls are refined and seek to be sated with some pure and heady sanctity. Torah holds the exact same aspiration just through a different instrument, but to identical ends. The message is the same but so much more, and the means of delivery is more subtle and "chall" (*takes a greater hold*). Being connected to it is what helps. The greater the demand on our time, the greater that renders the giving of it to learning the Gemara. It is then that you will recognize what you were doing prior as "less than". But as Moshe says there is nothing to say; perhaps because it touches on the only absolute, on the infinite, on the only real expansive inclusive. It's a shot in the soul of something. If we deeply don't know how to feel valuable, then we don't know how to handle being loved. Investing time in a Gemara addresses many issues from the inside. The more tethered to something spiritual – the more free a person is. And like all things, with freedom comes with a price. So choose the freedom you want, and the price you are prepared to pay.

It's a spa for the soul. Music speaks a similar language that people understand and, like the Gemara, can only present evidence to "open" minds, but there is no evidence "to open" minds, e.g. factual versus empirical distinction; observation from experience. It is worth distinguishing between conjecture and critical argument. Because also like all things, if you are looking to pull something down from a prejudicial conjecture you will surely think you have found something. But in the same breath, as a Jew you will surely find yourself, in the ultimate cathartic experience. The process is also a fabulous exercise in interrelation with others, also useful in performance.

Think of a great piece of music like Mahler's 5th. After learning a great Gemara, you will more recognize Mahler's genius, and enjoy his music more.

PROVISO

"He who has a why to live can bear almost any how."

Friedrich Nietzsche

Difficult things in life are always happening at the same time as good things. Most people in the world turn their head towards the bad things and allow them to obscure the good. But it is an active choice to turn your head towards the good. It won't make the bad, the sad, the difficult, or the troubling go away or make it better. But what you look at is up to you!

This could be called the "why" in Nietzsche's very famous quote. However, this "why" is an important point of consideration: Music or song or Gemora can be how you "turn your head to the good"; as it offers that place to feel alive when things are perhaps difficult. The dangerous upshot is, if overused, it can leave you not facing up to or attempting to deal with those difficult things.

Like personality
with no character,
always the fool.

And character
with no personality,
usually un-cool.

A bit of both,
is perhaps
the rule.

AUTHENTICITY

PAVAROTTI

Pavarotti made people feel like a friend. He has said some of the most inspiring things about singing and performance:

"I will not exist if I do not trust people."

"Singing is not a bluff, not a poker game – it's a chess game, you lose you don't have any excuse."

"A comedy about the triumph of sincerity."

"A strong diaphragm muscle to control the breath... they don't know that."

"Anyone who says he is not nervous before a performance is a liar."

And this is what Bono said about Pavarotti:

"humility is a mischievous trick" – but I'm sure Bono knows that for him it was no trick.

Bono also said how "each performance must have something of yourself in it, rather than being a facsimile of a past performance".

LADIES FIRST

For male performers, they say that getting the ladies on board usually means the men follow. Women have that deeper "6th sense" and are also more expressive, and so respond more visibly. So are more "with you from afar" as it were. Women also appreciate the courage to love and to express. You see that in reactions to songs like 'Woman' by John Lennon, which describes that courage. It helps to notice and focus on anyone who really appreciates what you're doing. In the back of your mind, perform for them. This helps increase the quality of your performance. You can give to them more if you ignore (inwardly) the more stoic audience members, male or female.

SING ALONG SONGS

The best way to invite people to sing with you, is to abruptly come off the keys, and stop singing, and let them take over.

WHAT PRICE AUTHENTICITY

I wrote the following after a good concert. It's a little abstract but I'm saying that even at the heights of the muse there are limitations. The goal is to not focus on them, but to plow through.

I found my way to the edge of the real
I can't turn back without grabbing the wheel
But my hands were tied from before I tried
to even out the deal
My circumstance is as you say,
but it's in the dance and as I play
It's where I am, and where I'm found
To love and believe is in the sound
This combination is somewhat rare
I know it's true, I know it's there
And all us souls who take the rains,
or pursue their goals
It's just the same, so don't forget,
we all get to choose that which we regret
So if I do complain or if I did abuse,
the rights I had, the rights I lose
And you along with them
I'm stubborn, and lucid, and wanton to burn,
including this page, my prisoner's wage
Coz I'm tired of what's average, I'm sick of what's old
Get me away from this savage, away from the bold
See me truly and simply, and all for the best
My life is amazing, I still have some left
No fear of referral, nor need of advice
Let go of your senses,
instead of your life!

THERAPY

FAILURE

At the moment when things go bad it looks or feels like failure, but failure really means: *trial and error and then don't think about why and what caused the "error", and don't plan to have it not happen again, and then don't try again* – (that would be called "trial and failure").

It is important to hone wherever you see the necessary legwork on your platform (*for you, not compared to anyone else*). That legwork will change what happened from a failure into an error.

Sometimes a failure can be the best thing that happens because it makes you stay in for a while and take stock, to practice and consider the above in a more relaxed way, but you can't plan these things – it's a divine design. We all are only ever partially the protagonists of our own life, but it helps to be forgiving of others as well as yourself, and it helps a lot to recognise the small successes. But it really helps the most to be stubborn, and take a portion of time for the thing you love (*for you*), the vocation, the career, whatever it is. And it is the "more responsible" thing to even steal time at the cost of something everyone else will tell you is the greater responsibility. So you will feel a bit guilty (*only if it's a bit!*). It is of crucial and far reaching importance to service what one really wants to achieve, of course seeing that it is realistic and possibile, *and that is nothing to do with money, and everything to do with being something of value to others, when shared.* So if the big dream looks to others as delusional, are there genuinely good enough small aspirations along the way? Then a relentless sense of perfection is always fun even if it takes time to be sure of an assessment. It's enough of an indication if you have had glimmers of your best here and there, where you managed to access a heightened better way of playing, with an audience, the operable word being *playing*. You may just want to get there sooner or more reliably, and to re-produce those great performances - when you get into "that mode" *see "First Song" section in the "Engagement" chapter earlier in the book.*

It's when you haven't seen the little successes (*fully realised aspirations in and of themselves*) that it's time to reassess. If you do, the best thing to always aim for is "some growth." When you see the response and what it does for people, that's meaning. And then failure becomes not as bad as *not doing* something challenging, worthwhile and exciting. You just want to avoid falling into the category of, I too had a dream—and killed the dream.

"It's important to fantasise sometimes, but if you do it to a point where it is too high or unreachable, then it will kill the original dream. Things take time. To whatever extent you do it, the fact should be that you just love to do it. And that's why you do it. Regardless of what amount of it you 'don't do.' You still love to experience it, from whatever angle or capacity, or degree of ability. Also focusing on what you hate to do, that you *have* to do, to 'get there.' That's not the way to get to it. That's what would kill it." -Mesoud Benasuly

ANGER

When you leave a gig with a horrible feeling because something (or a few things) went wrong, it will usually have been because you never managed to get over yourself. Invariably the lesson will have been that in some way, you went (not "got") angry no matter how subtly. People do not "get" angry, they "go" angry - it is a choice. The biggest people are attuned to not even be bothered in the first place.

Until you reach that level, regards whatever happened, lowering expectations takes strength. This includes not giving a sharp answer even when engaged in your thing. Doing something with a little humor is the best option when required. But if the temperament is still to get angry, then as the psychologists will tell you that sometimes a person has perhaps a need to get angry and is looking to fulfill that need. So, in that moment, "I don't deserve anything" is what you can try to tell yourself. But later, consider in your spiritual (not performance) life if you have enough things that bring you deep happiness. Things that involve some kind of charity, kindness, study, or prayer.

All said; "You cannot wake someone up who is pretending to be asleep." - Korean saying

SOLID GROUND

You still get the selfish dictator pretending to be unaware of people's feelings, even in a crowd, who needs to make negative comments at sensitive moments when everyone else is with you in some subtle or personal space.

You can be safe in the knowledge that most hecklers are known to be a pain elsewhere – it's good to bear in mind.

Still, be nice to them – safe in that knowledge. It's important to know you are on solid ground.

You can joke a bit at their expense, to a varying degree, while also complimenting. Some heckling can even help establish a relationship with the audience at large. And this is a good thing – so, what you do with it is important.

Remember, there is no such thing as "not fair".

You can and should give a huge berth avoiding any reaction to some, but if they persist or are overly disruptive to others, then you have an obligation to shut them down. So in the end it's up to you to prevent the few from ruining things for the many; that is if it gets to a point where the more you let them away with it the more brazen they become. Or if it starts at some extreme point of aggressive and loud, e.g., "Are we listening to this sh**". No sympathy is required. The trick is to deal with it before they get you down. If you don't, then the service you offer to the rest of the warm audience is compromised by allowing their negative disruptions.

In these cases you may have to go bigger and uglier to bring it round. Or find a security or authority figure and say, "Get them out of here. I've kindhearted people here to entertain. And I have someone too disruptive".

If it is as aggressive while at the same time more subtle,

and nonetheless disruptive, I have sung, in time and in tune to whatever I was playing at the time, "If you don't like it, you don't have to stay. If you don't like it, you know out is the way. I'm sorry I didn't do what you wanted me to, but the other people here, well the other people 'hear', what you seem to want to steer. So if you don't like it, don't stay, but why look at me that way…" Then I get back to the song with a renewed respect from my audience to whom I owe that service.

In the end, if you can be honest without going angry, that is the greatest wealth.

A CLEAR VIEW

Performance is a great place to learn about your better self because an audience can be both loving and unforgiving in a very truthful way. Even if the money is not so good, the payoff is still huge. Not only do you come out from under the cloud of whatever you are having a hard time with; willful blindness, rigidity, prejudices against you (*or ones you hold*) —but it also brings a strong natural drive to move forward in an accurate positive direction.

To be expressed is to "empty out" to where your natural instincts (always better) are more free to operate, in the moment. And so as the gig progresses you more and more recognise what it really means to share; the give and take.

You also come into yourself in a very true sense, and all things around you that are true are recognised, including a capacity for compassion which becomes much more relative. You get a clear view of the world and surpass many problems created by a lack of expression.

You are "rising above." See examples of perspectives that would be gained in a place like that—felt and understood— listed in "Parting thoughts."

But what is that switch that gets flicked, that caused you to become deeply creative and confident during and after a good gig? It is that you are no longer so self conscious. But why? It is because you opened up and expressed to a group of people, and were accepted. This is not a small thing. And so thereafter the more deep-seated hang-ups simply disappear into some wiser context naturally. This is being happy with who you are and what you are. While they are still different, and one does not excuse the other, but they enhance each other if you strive for both.

Mental health can be a state of mind
Don't think me rude or worse unkind
I mean to say try not to be blind
With expression you can change
and new perspectives find
It's not a quiz, or an intricate game,
It's safe never is
As doubt is the brother of shame

To make your music great you must work outside of it, to improve yourself in ways you are conscientiously aware of.

Then, in that audience relationship where you "let go" your voice, it comes from your spirit into the physical – that's to really sing, with trust, to allow it out, and then with trust they let you in, and you them. True solace is found in empathy with others and in learning.

This gives a person confidence and the power to express themselves, as well as satisfaction.

Having come from a difficult background many artists only find agreement with people eye to eye. Musicians may become performers, and also writers, because of a deep need to be heard having felt they were not and so had to muse, then it builds up, and the rest is history. To where being creative is an act of immunity out of control (free from), to where the musician can become the muse - to some extent.

In the world of modern entertainment, performance can seem like, "I have to be seen to be sure," but it's "I have to be sure to be seen," gives the strength in the long run. The former is true in many circumstances but doesn't offer a real position. You want to give people a reason for a connection with a song as well as a feeling.

POSITIVE DUALITY

"In art ... as in letters, what makes success is talent, and not
ideas ...The public understands the idea later. To achieve this
"later", the artist's talent must manifest itself in an agreeable
form and so ease the road for the public, not repel it from the
outset. Thus Auber, who had so much talent and few ideas,
was almost always understood, while Berlioz, who had genius
but no talent at all, was almost never understood."

Georges Bizet (1838–75)

PERFORMER AND/OR WRITER

Don't let inspiration fool you or rule you, let it tool you. In this regard it is important to have the equipment/technical ironed out prior to a performance because nothing so discombobulates. Also as a performer, it's best not to suppress the writer in you, and vice versa – you mustn't just be one over the other so as to avoid the extreme traits of both. The writer can get too hung up on rules, the performer not give them enough respect.

The writer as too precious, the performer too carefree. And it's amazing how arrogant a performer can be the day after a great show which he likley forgot was due to some profound sadness felt prior, giving way to a freedom to express in a more carefree manner.

"I suffer so much in this life. That is what they [the audience] are feeling when I sing, that is why they cry. People who felt nothing in this life cannot sing."

Enrico Caruso (1873–1921)

It's not to say don't specialise, but knowledge of your counterpart can make your game.

The positive side of broader experience is not to forget the focus, but to add a deeper understanding in what you want, so as to help you achieve it. Spend some time in your counterpart role to get a feel for the positives and negatives of both. In the same way that the logic of a piece gets through sometimes, or the emotion of it gets through - delivery involves a negotiation, a balance between the two as you travel through different songs.

An artist in the room is responding to, and/or intertwined with, what's happening with the people in the room, there is an exchange taking place. Don't be put off because music was highjacked by the DJs, so of course, there is a greater need than ever for live music and musicians. I have seen all ages responding in the most loving ways as to suggest that people crave live music and musicians. The DJ is to the musician, like the photographer to the painter; limited and compromised as an artist.

Every entertainer should be primarily an artist. This fluctuation happens in life as well as on the stage. Sometimes I'm an artist who knows a bit about how to entertain. Sometimes I'm an entertainer who knows a bit about art. But you can't get to be just "an artist" unless you vary the degrees of those two faculties—through a show and through everything you do.

Would thought kill action!?
If there was some greater satisfaction.
Perhaps to do is less than you.
Perhaps to consider
somehow bigger?
Writers are renowned
and remembered profound.
And actors only
give glory to their moment or story.
Adding light to their view
though without whom what would we do.
No, life is a blend, a balance refined
the journey is the end
then again it's inclined.

Being an artist is being true to yourself in your performance, however it suits you at the time. Entertaining is paying attention to people; giving to them, and caring about them.

You will never get to be an artist (and not a decent one either) without being a bit of an entertainer. You do this by paying attention to see if you are relating—and even chatting with your audience. That's called entertaining. You may want to be the artist, but you can't if you're not an entertainer.

You will still need to take risks in this. For example, some of the songs in the show should be a risk as to whether they will like them or not.

Chapter Five

AND AFTER

MÉMOIRS
and lessons learned

"When I am no longer here you will hear it said of my work: 'After all, that was nothing much to write home about!' You must not let that hurt or depress you. It is the way of the world ... There is always a moment of oblivion. But all that is of no importance. I did what I could ... now ... let G-d judge!"

Gabriel Fauré's last words to his sons (1845–1924)

MCDONALD'S

McDonald's *Brent Cross London.*

Many gigs offer a deal of insight into the world and the lives around you, where although you are the entertainment you get to observe a lot. Few have been like this one. Here are four stories from when I played in McDonald's Brent Cross, in London. I played five or six hours a day for about £6 per hour. A lovely lady Christina was my boss; she gave me a pen for X-mas and I still have it. At that time Brent Cross was the biggest shopping mall in Europe and McDonald's just wanted to do something different – hence the grand piano.

1: LAMB

A disabled girl in a wheelchair, about four feet in front of me who would make lamb bleating noises, a noise so essential in your being, as it seemed to me whenever the music got the most sensitive.

I knew if I drew attention to her by staring or letting it affect me it was going to make other people look too. It was up to me to not be a cause of embarrassment for the girl as well as the people looking after her.

LESSONS LEARNED

This was a deep exercise in not being distracted. It was hard to concentrate because someone disabled making a bleating sound like a lamb is a base sound from the very depths, very heartfelt, it's coming from somewhere even beyond. And hopefully an artistic expression is coming from somewhere deep or beyond, so you have to steel yourself but at the same time make yourself available – it was hard. The important lesson in ignoring certain things around you, as well as someone bleating, is when one person gets up and leaves; you mustn't draw attention to that either.

2: CHICKEN *(CLUCK STORY I)*

Second was the time when some kids were throwing hard sweets at me. This McDonald's was big and had a huge balcony overlooking a lower atrium with the piano in the middle. Someone was standing beside me with a request menu when something hit the paper, so they left in a hurry, then another one skimmed across the piano.

I couldn't see where it came from. I was a bit afraid, and with a little bravado, also concerned a bit about being seen as a coward if I left. I got on the microphone and announced "you know when somebody attacks you and you can't see them, and they are hiding behind a pillar or other people – what's that called again? Oh yes, a chicken." And I proceeded to make a clucking sound, and the people started laughing. And I'm looking upstairs and I see a group of kids round one guy who's not laughing, but all the others are – he's the guy that's throwing them. But I get to look him in the eye and kind of say with my eyes, "hey, you know I don't want to be your enemy," and smile. I didn't know if they were going to beat me up but they all came down and asked for requests for their girlfriends that were about to come out of the bathroom.

LESSONS LEARNED

In an antagonistic situation, try to quickly switch from the offensive to offering friendship. Stand up for yourself, but be prepared to go for peace as soon as possible.

It is worth noting that music has a great relaxing power. The more deeply relaxed a person is – the more you can pull that smile.

3: GRAN TORINO

The most personal and powerful story was a man who was crying during the Jamie Cullum song "Gran Torino". I had been paying semi-attention; I was playing six hours a day so there are moments when you're not really fully involved in a piece. So I saw this old man crying, but no one else could see that he was crying, and I could see that it was something to do with the lyrics. So I had to say to myself, "you better up your game; this means something very personal to him. Get focused and do a good job for this man."

I left my digital device recording for the whole day, so I have it recorded, and I recognise the moment when my attitude changed, and the place also got very quiet then too.

I made sure for the rest of the song I gave it it's due focus, and also not to let it be known that I had seen him cry. At the end a ripple of applause started on the balcony and worked its way round to the people sitting beside me.

LESSONS LEARNED Hear at: https://youtu.be/3fSyzEcXDNY

How to use feedback from the audience to enhance performance. And another exercise in not letting it be known that my attention had been distracted, but to a different extreme, where this time it was only me who was aware of it in the first place.

4: REGRET

Another story where I had to make sure to not divert attention, though it was only myself and a handful of people who were aware.

A father and son were sitting with their backs to me about 15 feet away, eating on the high stools at the thin eating shelf. The son was trying, it seemed, desperately to get his father's attention, then all of a sudden the man struck his son on the side of the head full force. The son's ear went immediately bright red, and it seemed instantaneously that the father now felt bad. The son was now holding his ear in pain and turned away, and now the father desperately wanted his son's attention and forgiveness, but the tables were turned and the son was completely ignoring him. And you just start thinking this is probably going to be perpetuated for generations to come, and it need not only be played out with physical violence.

LESSONS LEARNED

The similarity in the way the son and father were both desperate for each other's attention was an example, albeit extreme, of how the closer people are the more vicious cycles are difficult to recover from.

DR KHOO

...not the evil magnate from James Bond

Westfield shopping centre, *Shepherd's Bush, London. With Dr Khoo and his wife as he picked me up for a three year stint at The Corus Hyde Park.*

PART I

I had a slot playing on a beautiful Yamaha concert grand in the Westfield shopping centre, Shepherd's Bush London, in the Gucci/DKNY section. I wasn't paid at all by the centre but playing every Sunday I would pick up jobs like an engagement party out in Sussex at some country estate.

One day a gentleman came by and stood for a while with his wife as I played, then he asked me when I finished if I would go to his hotel, I assumed to meet with him at a hotel he was staying at in London's West End to discuss some one-off gig. But it was to *his* hotel, one of many he owned; he was Dr Tan Sri Khoo Kay Peng, a Malaysian businessman and chairman and major shareholder of Laura Ashley plc. as well as owning this hotel chain among other businesses.

I packed up my rig, got in the car and every two minutes my phone would ring with someone from his entourage asking if I was ok, if I knew the way etc. I arrived and his stretch Rolls Royce was at the door, and was told to park my van directly behind it. They opened the door for me, and standing at the door to meet me was the General Manager, Andrew Hollett, and a bunch of staff, all at attention. I was offered wine and chocolates as they welcomed me in.

I was then ushered downstairs to one of the hotel's restaurants "Bel Canto", an opera restaurant in the basement, where the "stars of tomorrow" from the London Opera school would serve your meal and every fifteen minutes break into song.

We sat and I played for two hours, me, the GM, Dr Khoo, his wife and an entourage of lawyers and bodyguards. He would sit beside me and try to join in on the piano at times and his touch was that of a sledgehammer, I had to encourage a perhaps more sensitive approach. Eventually I said, "okay so what's going on?" He switched into business mode and we sat at one of the big tables discussing a price for me to play three hours a night three nights a week (eventually it became four hours a night four nights a week, and for three years). Then Dr Khoo asked, "do we pay you more than Westfield?" I answered him honestly.

"Well, yes."

They did not yet have a grand piano up in the lounge and Andrew was instructed to get one in for me. But I could sense I was being "imposed" on the hotel by the chairman, and Andrew (we later became good friends) was none too pleased but could do nothing about it, except perhaps hope that when his boss was out of the country it could all be swept under the carpet. This was my only chance to cement the deal, so I asked Dr Khoo how long he was going to be around. He said only a few days. I said

"I bet you can't get the piano in for Tuesday. If you do, I will come in and do your last night here for free." He said, "I bet you I can!"

At the Corus

PART II *(CLUCK STORY II)*

The piano was placed at the top of the lounge above the spiral staircase that led down to the opera restaurant. Before I came along, they were used to keeping their restaurant door open so as to win the attention of passers by from the lounge area above. But two conflicting music sounds were very distressing for me, never mind that it can be disturbing for the people upstairs, so I asked that the door be kept closed. This was not received well by the restaurant manager. The GM asked them to keep it shut, but they would keep opening it.

Dr Khoo would visit at random times, so when he did I spoke to him about the problem, and it was all sorted, or so I thought. As soon as he was back in his jet and out of the country, the opera waiters gathered in the footwell, chose their moment and belted out this long opera note, loud and sustained for a ridiculous amount of time. I was in the middle of "New York State of Mind" by Billy Joel; the people around the piano looked shocked. I got a fright too, but I understood that they think they are not getting their usual business because of me. What can/will I do? If I complain to Dr Khoo again I'm going to be the moaning piano player because the restaurant is a busy money-making thing, but I can't do nothing because they will keep the door open and I can't cope with two musics at once, and it's such a well-paid job I can't lose it.

So I went downstairs and waited for them to be mid aria "Vissi D'arte", and I walked into the restaurant and walked up to each of the strategically placed singers who were around this big restaurant, and I looked each one in the face and gave them my now well rehearsed chicken clucking noise, then I went onto the next one. I went round all four of them, then went to the restaurant manager and said, *"keep your guys under control,"* gave a smile, hopefully a winning smile, and left.

The strategy, however, did not look like it was going so well this time as I immediately got a call from the GM telling me to pack up my stuff and leave for the night, just in case things escalate, and to come in the next day with a written report.

I go in the next day, without a written report. I sit in Andrew's office and he tells me off, and tells me I have to do a written report, but then at the end says "It was quite a funny story."

LESSONS LEARNED

My being at the Corus was primarily to raise the star rating of the hotel, and second to help sell drinks as well as help with repeat business. The discomfort of the guests was not the high priority of the hotel, albeit a concern, but two music sources at once was impossible to live with and this was a well-paid job so my performance had to be good. So it helps to know people at the top but you can't run with every problem, and to get Bel Canto "into more trouble" would have backfired because the opera restaurant is profitable. There was no choice but to take matters into my hands as best I knew how.

I am not advocating that whenever anybody gives you flak you must stand up to them. But if you do make sure you quickly try to turn it round to something pleasant, when you get the chance, to get them on your side.

I never made that written report (until now, I guess), they didn't do it again, they kept the door shut, and every time I bumped into them in the halls for the next two or three months I smiled as if to say "look, I don't want to be your enemy." Sure enough a few more months later the opera singers, when they finished their shift would come up and sit at the piano and make requests and have a drink, and I had a singalong with some of them, and that was nice.

It is worth noting that to embarrass someone is not a good thing to do. We are talking only about fighting fire with fire, and not where one has to be more respectful, e.g. in a family situation, but out in the world you have a bit more room.

Regards playing in Westfield for free, it has been a constant factor in my life that whenever I was out playing I got work by being out there. Even when I was not being paid, something would come from it.

SWEET AS PIE (IF YOU USE YOUR TEETH)

It's worth noting that reaching out to people in high places is useful at times, and do not be afraid to do it. It happened to me in the USA with a good customer. I performed for them many times, the crowd enjoyed me, and I enjoyed the crowd. I got on really well with the program director, but he left and a new person came in, and I got a bad attitude from the new person to where they were pushing me out of the situation. Perhaps they had their entertainers, but I had something good going there. At one point he hung up on me, it seemed, during a phone call while I was asking if I could I pop in and say hello. So at that point I found out the company owner's name and I called up and got his answering machine. I left a message saying, "I get on well with the people and the old program director, but the new person I think doesn't want me, so I probably won't be back. If you want to talk about it please call me." Sure enough, four hours later I got a call from the new program director and they were sweet as pie!

LESSON LEARNED

Importantly the lesson here was not to call up the boss with even an ounce of anything that could be construed as anger because I was hurt from being hung up on. If I had left even a slightly a nasty message and I even did get the job back it would be uncomfortable. It just had to be super straight. If you have good work invested in a place don't let it go so easily.

Café des Art's *with the Davidoff trio Basil*

HUGGING IN SWITZERLAND I

Café Des Arts, Basel

This was a cool place; so cool in fact it was freezing. I had to work extra hard to connect with the audience, but it was a great place and often Avo Uvezian of Davidoff Avo cigars would come in wearing his white suit, and with his Jazz trio and we'd play "Ain't No Sunshine" for half an hour.

At this gig there were some nights that were fantastic.

One of these nights I was playing "Piano Man", and indeed there was an old man sitting next to me with a gin and tonic, and in my imagination the scene in the Billy Joel anthem was unfolding around me. There were people sitting around the piano, and it was a fabulously warm buzzing humming along evening. But the place had seats behind me that I didn't notice. The music was piped throughout the sound system, and behind me in the corner on these cinema seats that they put into this artsy place, there was this guy under the speaker for the whole night that I never saw.

I had learned that when you are involved in a song, an intimate and shared idea, that the spaces between the songs, and what you talk about is a good place and time to balance things out in the audience relationship. Keep it light but still share interesting facts etc., just have a conversation. But that's when you can see all the people around you, and you get a feel for who they are/how they are responding. You have one guy surprised that you know this song, or asking how come you don't, or some woman who keeps asking for the same song, a bunch of different things, but you know where they are coming from. If they like you it's really nice etc., but there is a two-way relationship with naturally tempered boundaries. But not with someone you have not seen, or made any eye contact with, who feels close to you, helped along by being drunk. So at the end of the night when I finished, he came up from behind me, I didn't see him, and he gave me a hug, but it was with all of his heartfelt and intoxicated emotion.

LESSONS LEARNED

I learned how stunningly disturbing somebody you don't have a relationship with being physically and emotionally intimate with you can be.

Be aware of people who you cannot see, and that this may happen, especially if they are drunk.

The Chesa Grischuna *Klosters*

HUGGING IN SWITZERLAND II

Hotel Chesa Grischuna, Klosters

On the flip side of the hugging story in Café Des Art, was the hugging story in the Chesa Greschuna in Klosters, a ski resort where I was hired for six weeks. This was a hot spot for the rich and famous. I mostly met the hired help of the stars: the chef of Bill Gates who told me she had just cooked dinner for her boss along with John Travolta and Bill Clinton; Mariah Carey and Sean Connery's pilots; Bill Clinton's bodyguards. And Tara Palmer-Tomkinson was a regular customer at the piano.

So this guy would come in every day with an older lady and give me this deathly look. I smiled – but nothing! There was simply nothing to go on. And at the end of each song the guy would stare even more aggressively and then she would look at him with a smile. I wondered why do they come in? If you don't like me, if you don't like it – leave, or complain or something! I simply couldn't fathom it. This was before I met Mesoud and he encouraged me to deal better with people, so I was like "I'll show them." After a week of this torture, I brought in a camera in readiness. I waited for the nastiest look and pounced. I pulled out the camera and snapped their ugly mugs. The guy stood up, and I hadn't noticed before how big he was, he comes over towards me, I stand up, he put his arms out, he wrapped them around me, and hugged me. Such a sweet innocent hug. I remember how I sank into his big sweaty burgundy jumper.

So the Swiss are not known to be the most expressive, and experience has shown this to be true, but this man was the autistic son of the lady, and I somewhat misread the signs.

LESSONS LEARNED

Look at the people in the room and take a pool of how they feel in the majority; if the odd person has a terrible look, it's not necessarily how they feel. I have seen it other times, too. A woman once was laughing at me, and it felt horrible; turns out she was very nervous, but it struck me as mocking.

Don't judge a book by its cover. When you see people, you can misread them. A person's face is not always what they are.

Princess Square *Glasgow*

TELEPATHY

The first time was in Princess Square when someone came up to me and suggested I play "New York State of Mind" (coincidentally or not from the earlier story), and I was about to play it anyway. It happened more over the years and I found this really interesting. I wondered why is that happening now? What was in common with the other times, when I'm about to play a song and someone asks me for it.

This is more of an idea than a story. It seems limited to enclosed public spaces, like a hotel lounge or a fancy shopping centre. I can never fully prove it because it happens at moments of an extreme lack of self-awareness. You also have to have people who can choose to be close to you in their minds, where they have less "static" in their head than the other people who are rushing around (like the "Middle Phase"), perhaps it's because they are making an effort to focus on the music.

It also has to be when I'm deep in the music that someone would approach me to make the request, and at that moment I also happen to be near the end of the song, and in my head I'm selecting what to play next, and many times they request that exact song. Once I accidentally recognised the moment and called them on it before they had the chance to speak, and I was right.

But to have the jump on yourself in this situation is extremely difficult because you can't be that self-aware when you are that involved in the music, and still be aware that this is that kind of moment and perhaps this person is going to ask for that song that you are thinking of playing.

LESSONS LEARNED

Melody without words can carry meaning, a simple example being "Yesterday" by the Beatles. (Without the words, the melody metaphorically says the same thing). My theory is a bigger leap, but that in some way music can carry a specific thought, in that while you are playing, with all the above circumstances in place, a thought can carry through the room, and people can pick up on that somehow, the channel is opened through the music. Perhaps it is that thoughts can be carried when a deep common focus is engaged, and telepathy can exist, music being an opening to a collective unconscious.

I like to think so.

Bastille Taverne *Glasgow with Rich on drums*

RICH ON DRUMS

The Bastille was a bar in Glasgow owned by Colin Bar who got me and a very funny friend Rich on drums in to play. We were squashed together, his back was pressed against my left arm. One night we played Elton John's "Benny and the Jets". The bar was packed with people also up against us with drinks spilling on the upright piano and the drums.

The room was humming along nicely and on this song we got really into it and were getting louder than the room, and then we slowed it right down and we both noticed this massively busy bar was listening to everything we were doing, only I couldn't contain it and started laughing. For a moment though, the hubbub came in line with us and the whole packed bar wall to wall got quiet.

LESSONS LEARNED

I was (and still am) embarrassed at having such sincere attention, so "holding" that holy grail was impossible, so I laughed and lost it and the talking resumed.

It was that exquisite moment where everyone in the place at the exact same time feels that their conversation isn't quite as interesting for a moment as what the guys in the corner playing piano and drums are doing. That was the moment I remember first thinking I really want to get better at this.

Hopefully I'm a bit less embarrassed about these things now and there's different ways of working with them now.

Self portrait

WONDERING

The "Rich on drums" story was on the eve of a Jewish high holiday where even the most disenfranchised go to shul (synagogue).

There was a kollel (group of Talmudic scholars) in the basement of Giffnock shul, that back in the day was busy on these holidays. Rabbi Bamberger who funded the kollel had made a rule that these guys deep into Talmudic study should not separate themselves at these times and should be seen, and mingle a bit so people can get to know them and perhaps want to learn with them. He also told them when you are up there with everyone don't gather in a clique either, so they were placed around the room.

I came late after this great gig and was on a high. It had been a special time musically, which is an elevated spiritual thing so I was somehow able to see "further ahead". I looked around and remember well how I could pick them all out. These guys in black and white and they all seemed to be doing the same thing / in the same place, all concentrated in whatever they were doing amidst people who were talking here and there. It looked authentic to me and I kept looking and looking and wondering, "what are they doing, what's it all about?!"

This was the first thing that started my interest in observant Judaism, along with Rabbi Jacobs from Chabad, and Garry Mann introducing me to these guys in the Kollel.

LESSONS LEARNED

It takes one vantage point to recognize another.

With a real piano in the River Kelvin, Glasgow

A LONG "WALKING IN MEMPHIS"

There was a guy sitting beside me, a rather robust fellow with the Nazi "SS" symbol tattooed on his neck. And in came someone who appeared to be his boss. They looked to be a part of some Eastern European mafia syndicate. There were big thick bundles of cash and girls all over the place. The boss told a joke and everyone laughed. The boss put £50 on the piano and said play, "Walking in Memphis" by Marc Cohen (a Jewish singer-songwriter). So I played it, and I got to the end of the song and the guy with the SS on his neck turned round to me and said, "play it again." I got to the end of it again, and again he said, "play it again." I started to think to myself that this is what it must have felt like for the poor Jewish people who were made to play violin for the Nazis. So, it wasn't that extreme a situation, but I was a bit afraid to not do well musically and put my heart into something, and stay afloat for these people.

LESSONS LEARNED

I guess the lesson is even in extreme situations you can find a way to serve a memory of some kind.

NOT SO SINATRA

I did a regular Sinatra tribute every Sunday, "his food, his drinks, his music". Veal parmesan, a Jack Daniels, and I'd sing "My Way" twenty times. There was a fellow who waited till the end, and Mesoud had just been trying to get it through to me that when people have a complaint don't react so fast, listen to them, and tell them you've heard them. So this was my big chance to see if it worked. He had been watching me all night sitting on his own, so he comes up to me and says, "it's clear the people like what you are doing but it's billed as a Sinatra night and you are not singing at all like Sinatra." He went on for a solid three minutes. I steeled myself and listened while aching to say "I'm doing it My Way," but I didn't, I said, "I hear you, I hear what you've had to say." That was it, that was all I said. He had a grin on his face from ear to ear.

LESSONS LEARNED

Doing music is something you hopefully get into and is something you are enjoying, and so is inevitably shared. The spaces between are the more tricky but you can learn to navigate them a bit, but that gets misread all the time as if you hold that impossible holy grail of being able to hold court, and he thought that's what I had, and he's on his own. So when he comes up to make a complaint about something, and I say I've heard him, I'm really answering the question that needs to be answered for him which is "can somebody hear me because I'm spending so much time in my own head?" So that was thanks to Mesoud's good advice.

We all want to be heard or witnessed, and if you ever momentarily hold that coveted spotlight then all you have to do is acknowledge that you have also heard, and you do a great kindness ... but don't be too sweet, coz people will want to eat you!

Photograph by Rosa De La Losa at the Corus

GIVING IN TO WIN

I'm adding in one story which involves disaster and failure. Everybody wants to hear those kinds of stories! There is a great lesson when you recognise failure, and double failure is worse. That's when you know something and you still get it wrong, which is such a human characteristic. But it is really important to recognise it.

It happened to me when I did a show in Glasgow and some people I kind of knew wanted in without paying. At the same time, there was a fault with the equipment at the front desk so they called me over. It was about 15 minutes before the show was going to start and I felt like my friends are being a little sly, and I began to get judgmental and a bit annoyed. So I got involved and bogged down in the technology of the payment system which I had implemented and put together. This had happened to me in a roundabout way once before so I already knew not to get involved with anything other than entertaining several minutes before a performance.

So much so I should have gone into my pocket and said, "not only do I want you to come in for nothing but thanks for coming—here's a hundred quid!" I'm exaggerating but the point is to go the other way rather than get bogged down in detail for the wrong reason and at the wrong time. And then I still couldn't get it fixed. By the time I was to go on to perform I was a zillion miles from where I should have been mentally. It took me 45 minutes to catch up with myself—45 minutes of below-average playing, and below-average interaction with the audience.

LESSONS LEARNED

One has to understand the priority. And the priority is the performance and the longevity, and the longevity is from the interaction, and the interaction is in the entertainment.

The mindset of interaction is very different from technical detail. We are all capable of both but you need to allow for the time and the place. That's why a half-hour buffer with nothing to do is essential. I hope, I hope, I hope I've learned that now!

If you are close to starting a performance you must refuse to deal with anything else. Instead, be prepared to fully "lose out" on whatever that situation is—you will win out in the long run. So, good luck! Another lesson is try not to do everything yourself.

That said, when important equipment needed for the actual performance goes wrong, even 30 seconds into the first song—don't cry or fret. Just fix it. Don't muddle through with broken equipment; stop! And if it can be done fairly quickly, fix it. Many people say carry on without it— rubbish! Just go about it as if to infer that fixing equipment is something worth watching, and chat while you do it.

PARTING THOUGHTS

Often when I finish playing I've got a lot of energy and can't sleep. So I play some more, write, or draw in one line where I don't lift the pen off the paper. Below are some ideas from those times.

Love Billy

These extra tips and tricks are to help serve, and should not lose sight of the main job, which is your interpretation of the song and the lyric. It's always about the song.

"Playing the game is better than winning the game."

"Having an excuse may not be an excuse."

"Just coz yawl seen a lot of things don't mean there aint' nothin new to see. And just coz you don't understand it don't mean it's wrong."

"May your needs and wants find harmony in your will."

• • •

"There are easier and more difficult truths."

"A hero is a man who battles his inner world to maintain a line that he knows to be the most refined."

"The only thing stronger than leverage is momentum."

"The definition of success is how much you can live with truth.
And the measure of failure, is how much you lie."

"Love is not a solution, it's a prize."

"In your greatest moment of deep inner turmoil, if you can calm yourself you will discover great things."

"Our wisdom is our strength, our reality our teacher."

"A good friend is a good critique as well."

"The way to learn from successful people is to hear repeated something you found out yourself, or somehow feel you already knew – so that what you now heard is a backup. As

Levi Yitzchak Nussen says, "You get two kinds of people – the one who memorized the timetable and the guy who took the train."

"Young people in all their goals would *do so much better* to listen to old people; old people would *be so much happier* to hear the young."

"You must stop listening to other people to listen to yourself. And stop making excuses for other people, including yourself."

"Being humbled before G-d is the most natural, peaceful state you can be in, and the first principle behind the driving force to your greatest success."

Paul Toshner, 1968–

"Playing a song is like in playing golf or shooting pool, if you take a somewhat "distance attachment" approach, you pot more frequently. All the better when combined with "a dose of judgement", and is best if you can simultaneously apply "care"."

Paul Toshner, 1968–

"NOW THROW THIS BOOK AWAY"

(or give it to a friend)

Not only will I be able to profit on the re-purchase – but importantly, you won't become obsessive over detail – like I have to fight from being all the time.

Lastly, be careful to define your act as accurately as you can. The following words took a while to come to, but people need a limited indication of what you do, even if you have a broad repertoire.

ABOUT THE AUTHOR

Princess Square *Glasgow*

Concert performer, author, and songwriter.

PLAUSIBLE INTERPRETATION a show by: Baby Tosh

Blending; jazz, classical and live looping versions of the 1970s New York Jewish singer-songwriters, as well as his own compositions. Performing in jazz clubs, community theatres, recital rooms, country clubs and home concerts.

Baby Tosh (aka Paul Toshner) is a singing pianist with a rich history as an artist across the globe. Musically, Paul delivers a unique art; blending classical and jazz piano with acoustic looping.

His book *Life is Grand, Baby! - Notes on Performance* is a culmination of discovery and feedback, with parallels to everyday people skills. Paul shares modes of understanding, both technically and spiritually in his book, along with memoirs and insights on the intimate performance of song from a real-life Piano Man.

Born to a businessman and an aerobics instructor, and very much part of mainstream society, at age 27, Paul decided to try a new kind of life. His quest for experience and understanding transformed him, taking him over oceans and across continents, to piano bars and community halls in London, Switzerland, Denmark, China, and the USA, as well as Yeshivas in New York and Jerusalem.

Paul was born in Glasgow, Scotland. He started life as a musician playing piano in Princess Square, a classy shopping center. Then moved on to hotel piano bars, where he once got to cover for a job in Denmark for a friend who couldn't make it. There he met an agent. From there, he went on to piano bars and ski resorts in Klosters and St. Moritz, Switzerland. Then residencies in two top hotels in London's West End. Followed by concert work for retirement communities, country clubs, 55+, piano shops, senior living, and various community centers in the USA.

His book is ostensibly for the frontman or the soloist. Someone who takes responsibility for the flow, pace, structure, material selection, engagement, and many dynamics relating to the audience relationship. It addresses the need to be concerned with the way something is delivered as much as what and where it is being delivered.

Thank you

ACKNOWLEDGMENTS

Thanks to:
Hashem
Tamar, Mum and Dad
Mesoud Benasuly and Tuli Dubiner
Libby and Levi Yitzchak Nussen
Eli Gestetner
Rabbi Yossi Galandauer and Shauly Jacobs
Yisroel Ament and Moshe Siegal
Everyone at Ger Golders Green

Sponsored by fans and friends,
from the London and New York kehilas
Including: Stephen and Debbie Goldberg, Heshy
Greensweig, Chaim Shulem Hechel, Yoichy Herzog, Heshy
Israel, Chaim Neiman, Shabsy Parness, Shmilu Schlesinger,
Rudi Sternschein, David E Weingarten
Voice coach: Lidea De Rosa
Piano teacher: Jim McDowall
Editorial support: Eli Gestetner & Josh Rivedal
Everyone who enjoys my show
And all the people who book me